NIKKI

GEORGE SHERMAN HUDSON

STREET CHRONICLES

DEC 2013

Join us on our social networks

Like us on Facebook: G Street Chronicles
Follow us on Twitter: @GStreetChronicl
Follow us on Instagram: gstreetchronicles

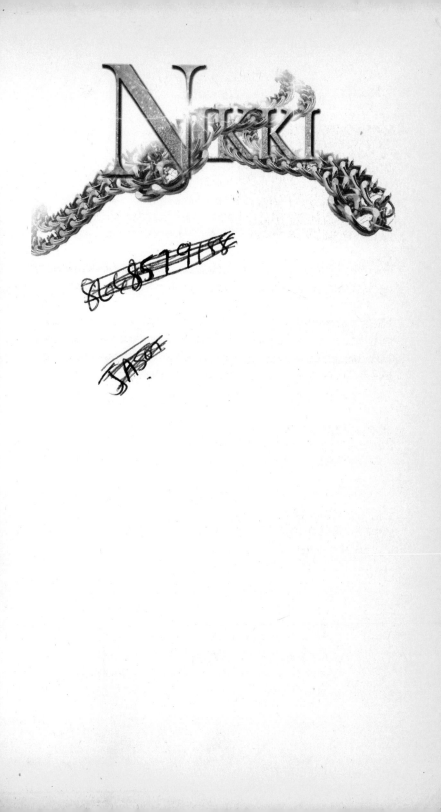

This book is dedicated to my li'l man,
my grandson Greyson...
the newest li'l member of the family...
put your tongue in your mouth!
Love ya!

Acknowledgements

First I want to acknowledge GOD…only through Him is this all possible.

Shout out to Mom and Pop (Lois & George), my family the Walkers, Hudsons and Adams!

To Shawna A., the hardest working woman in the industry who makes the impossible possible. You are a true soldier, ride or die, hustler, boss, motivator, fighter and on top of all of that, a true Queen. Not to mention your sidekick and my partner Tressa (Ma), the real BOSS! You keep me laughing.

To my son and daughter, Sherman & Jazmine, I'm proud of both of y'all…the next generation.

To the G Street family: We're on a mission and best believe we're not stopping until it's accomplished. In every war you have casualties so it's inevitable that everybody who started off will finish. I encourage everyone to strap up, grab your pen and go hard. Stand tall because if you fall you will be easily stumped by the opposition and easily forgotten in this industry that's growing by the day.

Much love to all the readers! Y'all make us who we are…A Publishing Powerhouse! We really appreciate y'all!

PROLOGUE

"I said lay down and don't fuckin' move!" the masked man screamed as he held my parents and me at gunpoint.

I was dealt a bad hand at birth. My dad was a corner hustler, and my mom was a low-class stripper who would easily sell the pussy as long as the price was right.

"Look, playa, just be easy," my dad said calmly, as he and Mom lay facedown on the dirty carpet that covered the floor in our run-down apartment.

The masked man had to be a crack fiend, because our government housing would have been the last place anyone would have come to steal any real money. Shit, my dad was a nickel-and-dime nigga, and my mama didn't make much stripping and tricking.

I stood in the corner, shaking like a leaf on a tree, scared as hell.

"Please, mister, just take what you want and go, damn it!" my mother screamed, looking back over her shoulder at the intruder.

The junkie's hand shook nervously as he held the pistol on my mom and dad. "Where the rest of the money at?" he demanded. "I know y'all got more than this! Where the dope at?" he screamed, looking down at the measly $130 and two dime rocks my dad had handed to him when he'd first busted our door down.

My dad reached in both of his pockets and pulled them out like rabbit ears to show the robber that he didn't have any more money or drugs.

Disgruntled by his take, he walked over and snatched me from the corner. "I'ma kill this here li'l girl if y'all don't come clean!" he screamed, then shoved the barrel of his .38 revolver in my mouth.

"Please! No, man! I swear that's all we got!" my dad yelled, looking me in the eyes.

Out of nowhere, my mother jumped up, disturbed that somebody had a gun pointed in her baby's mouth. Even though my parents weren't the most positive role models or upstanding citizens, they had always loved me unconditionally, so sometimes, I still blame myself for what went on that day. My mama loved me so much that she couldn't help rushing toward that man and screaming, "Get your hands off my baby!"

Boom!

The gun blast pierced my young ears, leaving me partially deaf in one ear. The slug hit my mother in the chest, stopping her in her tracks.

"Nooo!" my father screamed, rising up from the floor.

The masked man held me with one hand while leveling the gun at my dad with the other.

Boom! Boom!

He pulled the trigger twice, killing my dad instantly. After my father collapsed to the floor, our attacker turned the gun on me. He stared at me with sinister eyes that I would forever see in my nightmares. My heart skipped a beat as the gun clicked, then clicked again; come to find out, the crack fiend only had three bullets loaded in his six-shooter, and he'd used them all up on my mama and daddy. He pulled back and cracked me over the head with the gun, knocking me out cold.

When I woke up an hour later, lying right next to my dead parents, I wasn't sure what to do, so I ran to the neighbors for help.

From being born with my umbilical cord around my neck to my parents' murders, I'd experienced some really fucked-up moments in life. That day just happened to be one of the worst.

CHAPTER 1

Years later…

Life is a journey, and mine had been filled with good and bad times. It all started after my parents were killed when my aunt, my mama's sister, took me in. Aunt Mattie was a God-fearing woman who practically lived in the church. Her fiancé, a man I referred to as "Uncle Gary," was a shade tree mechanic who worked on cars all day and nursed a liquor bottle at night. They raised me like their own, right up until my highly developed ass and plump tits got Gary's attention. I still laugh when I think back on the day when my Aunt Mattie jerked the door open and caught the two of us fucking like dogs in heat. Of course it had all started years before she caught us. I was fourteen and hot in the ass, and Uncle Gary was in his late thirties and fine as hell. He didn't have to rape me; it was all consensual.

The first time we went there, I couldn't wait for him to get drunk after my aunt left for her nightly Bible study. I crept into his room, naked as the day I'd come into the world. I was young, but I also knew the power of a well-developed body and young pussy, somethin' my prostitutin' mama had taught me. Besides that, hanging with my older hood-rat friends, Katasha and Fat Fat, had taught me a lot. My first lesson was to use what I had to get whatever I wanted, and Uncle Gary was my first trick.

"Girl, what you doing?" he called from his recliner, surprised to see me standing in his room with nothing on.

"Nothin'," I said, all innocent and shit, as if walking around like that was perfectly normal. I could tell by the look in his eyes that he wanted some of my young, ripe pussy, but little did he know that he was about to be my first. A new outfit and a couple dollars would be well worth it.

"What's going on, Nikki?" he asked, looking at me hungrily while taking a sip of the vodka from the red plastic cup in his hand.

I stood back on my young bow legs like I'd seen Fat Fat do when an attractive man came on the scene. I then ran my hands over the curves of my well-developed body until I reached my hairless privates. "I'm just tryin' to see what that's all about," I said, dropping my eyes to the growing bulge in his sweatpants.

The game Katasha and Fat Fat had taught me played right out before my eyes. He set the cup down beside the recliner and ran his hand over his hard dick. Seeing how far his pants stood out had me kind of scared, but I knew if whole babies, heads and all, came out of pussy, his dick wouldn't be a problem. I walked over and stood directly in front of him.

"Talking about this?" he slurred, pulling his dick out so I could see it.

"Yep." I swallowed hard, knowing I'd gone too far to back out.

He stood up, grabbed my wrist, and led me over to my aunt's bed. I climbed up on the bed in front of him, making sure to give him a good look at what he was about to get. I lay on my back and spread my legs wide, then began slowly stroking my pussy like I'd seen on the pornos I used to sneak and watch.

"Mmm…" I moaned as my uncle buried his head between my legs and started flicking his tongue across my clit. I will never forget how good that shit felt. From that day on, a nigga would have to lick the clit before he hit.

A few minutes later, he was butt-ass naked on top of me.

At the age of fourteen, I had the body of a grown woman, but when my uncle entered me, I realized I was still a child and definitely a virgin. "Damn!" I screamed, digging my Lee Press-On Nails in his back.

"Oh yeah," he said, grunting as he slowly slid his big package inside of my small hole, taking my virginity.

The pain was unbearable for the first few minutes, but then the pain turned to pleasure. My young pussy wrapped around his dick like a tight glove, and by the way he was moaning and calling out my name, it was as if I had the best stuff in the world. As he pounded away, I thought back on how Katasha and Fat Fat used to tell me that young pussy would have old niggas whipped. I wanted to make sure I had Uncle Gary eating out of the palm of my hand after our little session. I went at it like a pro, simulating everything I'd seen on the porno. I threw it back to him, turned it around for him, then rode him like a porn star.

"Oh, Lawdy! Shit! Fuuuuck!" He scrunched his face up as he shot his hot nut into me.

After he came, he held me like a kid cuddling his favorite

teddy bear.

From that day on, I got whatever I wanted from my uncle, but it all came to an abrupt end two years later. I was seventeen, about to turn eighteen, when I came to the end of my road. I was thick as hell, rocking the flyest gear, and carrying a Coach purse full of tens and twenties. I was the shit! Before long, I lost interest in school and dropped out. My aunt was so tied up with the church and other religious duties that she didn't even notice. My uncle didn't care, as long as I served him his young pussy fix on the regular.

It was Friday, and I needed an extra $200 for a Baby Phat outfit I'd seen in the mall. Instead of waiting for my aunt to head out to Bible study that night, I cornered my uncle early in the day, before she got off work.

"What up, sexy?" I said, licking my lips as I stood at the door.

"Shit. Gotta pull a motor for old lady Jones. I don't know why she just don't get rid of that old piece of junk. Mattie still at work?" he asked, picking up on my gestures.

"Yeah. I need you to help me out though," I said, looking up at him with my big brown eyes.

He walked over, wrapped his arms around me, and grabbed a handful of my ass. "What you need help with, baby?" He leaned in and kissed me on the neck.

"I need $200," I said, reaching down to rub his dick. I knew money was getting tight around the house because of me, but I didn't care, as long as I got mine.

"Damn, Nikki. You gon' have to wait till I finish Mrs. Jones's car. I'll give you $300 then," he said, running his hands over my hardened nipples that stood erect under my thin, tight t-shirt.

"Wait? Nah, that's a'ight. Forget it. I'll just get it from

somebody else. I gotta go. Move!" I snapped, pushing him off me.

He grabbed my arm as I started to walk away. "A'ight, Nikki. Damn!" he yelled, then reached in his pocket and pulled out a wad of money. He peeled off the $200 I'd asked for and held it out to me. "Here."

"Thanks," I walked back up to him and pressed my body against his.

He lifted me up with ease and carried me up to his and my aunt's bedroom. I was butt naked, drenched in sweat, riding him like a jockey, and screaming his name when the bedroom door swung open.

"Oh my God! I rebuke thee! You little whore! What are you doing? God help me, Jesus! Get out of my house!" she screamed at me as if I was the only one in the wrong.

Uncle Gary pushed me off him and pulled the covers up around him like a little bitch as my aunt yelled and screamed at me.

I jumped up, grabbed my clothes, and ran out of the room.

Seconds later, my aunt burst into my room. "I can't believe you! I took you in and raised you like my own, and you seduced my man? You got ten minutes to pack your stuff and get out of my house! I don't care where you go or what you do. Ten minutes!" she screamed, then turned and stormed out the room.

While I was packing my stuff, I heard her yelling at my uncle in the other room. I quickly grabbed all I could, then lifted my mattress and grabbed my stash. Katasha had warned me to keep one, just in case of emergencies, and I was glad I'd listened to her. I counted the wad of money and hoped the $2,800 would hold me over till I came up with a plan. I added the other $200 to it and stuffed it all in my sock, then grabbed my bag of clothes and shoes and left.

I kind of felt bad for Aunt Mattie because she had a no-good man, but as for my actions, I felt like I'd only done what I was supposed to do; I was sure nobody could fault me for that. I heard footsteps coming fast from behind me as I headed to the front door.

"Your time is up. I'm calling the law!" she screamed, holding the cordless phone.

"I'm out!" I snatched the front door open and stepped out in the cold Chicago air.

That was the day my life changed.

CHAPTER 2

"**D**amn, bitch, take it easy back there!" Katasha told Fat Fat as she ran the hot comb through the back of her hair.

"Ho, this shit nappy as hell. Next time, I'ma charge you double for this nappy-ass shit," Fat Fat said as she continued to straighten Katasha's hair.

Katasha and Fat Fat shared an apartment on Chicago's west side, a few miles from my aunt's crib. I had been hanging out at their apartment after school for a little over a year. I had met them one day when I was confronting a disrespectful little hoochie. When they saw me putting the young bitch in her place right in front of their apartment, Katasha and Fat Fat decided to take me under their wing. They really took a liking to me instantly, and since that day, they'd been teaching me everything they knew about the streets and the fast life. They really embraced me when they found out I always kept money for weed and liquor, being that they were always broke. Katasha and Fat Fat were two bad bitches who'd fallen on hard times after getting hooked on the new drug of choice, Mollies. They had even started lacing their blunts with cocaine. Despite their drug habit, they were both game tight, ex-strippers who had a lot of valuable lessons to share with me daily. I soaked up every drop of game that came my way. I knew they were on point because everything they told me happened just like they said it would.

As I walked down Third Avenue in the cold, I thought about my life and what was next. I'd been tossed out into the big, cold world all alone, left homeless. I knew my girls would let me stay with them until I put a plan together.

Knock! Knock!

"Who the hell that is? It better not be Cory, unless he's got a good excuse why his baby-mama keeps textin' me." Fat Fat laid the hot comb down and headed to the front to the door. She pulled the door open and positioned both her hands on her wide hips, then looked down at me. "Girl, what you doin' out here in the cold with that bag, all half-dressed and shit?" she asked.

I was standing on their front stoop in a pair of coochie cutters, a t-shirt, and a windbreaker. Until that moment, I hadn't even realized my lack of clothing; I'd rushed out of my aunt's crib so fast that I hadn't paid much attention. Now that Fat Fat was questioning me about it, I was suddenly cold as hell. "Damn, you gonna let me in or what?" I blurted out, then just walked around her into their small, cramped, one-bedroom apartment.

Fat Fat and Katasha had grown up on the rough streets of the Chi. They'd given up the stripper pole for tricking and selling drugs, the same drugs they both were now hooked on. They used to be the talk of the city, until their constant drug use broke them down and ruined their looks.

"Girl, who is that? Close the damn door. It's cold as hell out there!" Katasha screamed from the chair in the kitchen, where she was waiting for Fat Fat to come back and finish her hair.

I stepped in the doorway before Fat Fat could answer. "What up, diva?" I said playfully.

She looked me up and down. "Damn, bitch. What the hell you got on? What's in the bag?" she asked, looking at me like I was crazy.

"I was in a rush to leave my aunt's crib. She kicked my ass out," I said as the heat from the kitchen started warming me up.

"Kicked you out? You telling me Ms. Holier-than-Thou tossed your ass out the do'? Don't tell me she found out about you and—"

"Yeah, Gary," I said, taking the words right out of her mouth. I had told them about Gary a long time ago, and up until that point, everything they'd told me to do had worked.

"Damn, she found out!" Katasha said, positioning herself to listen in on all the drama.

"Worse than that, she caught us fucking!" I said, as if what I'd done was cool.

"Dat's fucked up! What'd she do?" Katasha asked as Fat Fat held the hot comb over the fire on the gas stove.

"Bitch, like I told you, she put me out. She even threatened to call the police on me if I didn't get outta her place. I packed whatever shit I could and got the hell out as fast as I could," I explained, rubbing my hands over my legs to warm them up.

"So where you goin' now?" Fat Fat asked, carefully pulling the hot comb through Katasha's hair.

The question made my heart flutter because it reminded me again that I really was homeless. "I, uh…well, I thought maybe I could crash here until I find me a place to stay," I said, dropping my bag to the floor.

Neither of them said a word, as if they hadn't heard me, and I couldn't believe my girls wouldn't offer me a place to stay.

"I could use my stash to keep up some good smoke and pills…or is it a problem for me to crash here a minute?"

The mention of the pills and weed got their attention, just like I knew it would; there was no way either of them could turn down a free high.

"Hell yea, girl! You know you can stay here till you get right," Fat Fat said while reheating the comb.

"It's all good, girl. Just find a spot in the front somewhere," Katasha added.

* * * * *

The days that followed were a blur. Most of the time, I was high on pills and weed. In just two short weeks, my money and my welcome had dwindled down to almost nothing.

"Girl, you found somewhere to go yet? Them front office people been complaining about too many people staying here," Katasha lied, trying her best to keep a straight face.

I couldn't believe Katasha would lie to me through her teeth while Fat Fat stood there like the shit she was saying was true. *Lies, huh? Well, two can play at that game.* "Yeah, I've got something lined up. I'll be outta here by the weekend," I lied. I rolled my eyes and turned away from them, looking down at my cell phone like I had a call. It was really difficult to hold my anger in. I couldn't believe the two bitches I trusted most in the world had used me and were now trying to kick me out just because my money was almost gone. *Damn. Don't friendship count for somethin'?*

"Oh okay, 'cause we ain't trying to get put out. Ya feel me, girl. You know how them Indian folks in the rent office are," Katasha said, then shot Fat Fat a sideways glance.

"Yeah, I know how they are with they're funny-acting asses," I played along, still pissed that I'd been played.

"Hey, I got company comin' over in about an hour, so y'all need to disappear in the back till he gone," Fat Fat said, cleaning up the front room.

I knew she was expecting a trick, but her logic really confused me. She refused to let a nigga fuck her in the bed because she somehow felt like that would be disrespectful to her man who was doing a five-year bid, but fucking a nigga on the couch for money was all right. The more I stayed around them, the more I realized they weren't as sharp as I thought.

"I'll holla at y'all, 'cause I'm 'bout to go get it in wit' my boo," Katasha said, grabbing her jacket and getting ready to go a couple doors down to Drew, her dope-head boyfriend's spot.

I went in the kitchen, made a sandwich, and headed to the back, out of sight.

A few minutes later, someone was knocking on the door.

"Who is it?" Fat Fat called from the bathroom, even though she already knew it was Trent, one of Chicago's big-time dealers.

Trent and Fat Fat had met a couple years earlier, when Fat Fat was a stripper at Dance Elite. Their introduction was more like a business deal: He offered her money for some ass. She told him what she charged, he paid, and they fucked. Even after Fat Fat had lost all her appeal and swag, he still kept coming back. Trent was a fine-ass nigga who had his pick of women, so I couldn't understand what kept him coming back to pay Fat Fat for her worn-out ass.

"It's Trent! Girl, open the damn door. It's cold as hell out here!" he screamed, looking around and hoping no one would see him heading into the apartment of two of the biggest tricks in the area.

Fat Fat rushed out of the bathroom to answer the door.

Meanwhile, I sat in the bedroom, stressing like hell and trying to come up with a plan.

About five minutes later, Fat Fat opened the bedroom door and stepped in. "Nikki, I need to get in here," she said, rushing through the room and picking up clothes.

"A'ight," I replied with a slight attitude. I stepped around her as she stuffed dirty clothes in her dresser.

Trent's eyes widened when I walked in front of him in my booty shorts and tank-top. I had seen the same look in his eyes on previous visits. I knew for a fact that I could have had my way with Trent and played him like I'd played Uncle Gary for so long, but I kept my eyes to myself and found a spot on the couch.

He stood, tucked his gun in his waistband, then gave me a hard glance before heading to the back.

Fat Fat closed the room door behind him, then turned on the radio.

Minutes later, I heard loud moaning and the headboard bumping up against the wall. *I guess respect don't mean shit when your man's off doin' a bid,* I thought to myself. I sat back on the couch, deep in thought, and looked around the shabbily furnished apartment. My eyes followed a baby roach as it skittered across the coffee table, and then it hit me. Trent's car keys were lying there, right next to his cell phone. I hesitated for only a moment, then got up from the couch and grabbed the keys from the table.

"Oh yes! Trent, get this punanny!" Fat Fat screamed from the back room as if he had the greatest dick in the whole damn world.

I grabbed my bag and my cell phone. I only had $120 to my name, but I didn't care. I picked up his leather bomber jacket off the chair, put it on, and slipped out the door. I climbed behind the wheel of his Dodge Challenger and brought the engine to life. The dual pipes growled, and the engine rumbled underneath me. I hoped he was too into Fat Fat to hear the roar of his car. I didn't have my license, but I wasn't exactly a novice behind the wheel either. I threw the car in drive and pulled out of the lot. I pulled up his navigation system and entered my destination, the ATL. Little did I know that Trent had $10,000 and ten kilos in the trunk.

CHAPTER 3

"Fat Fat!" Katasha called out as she entered the apartment a couple hours later.

She closed the front door and flipped the lights on in the pitch-dark front room. Her heart dropped when she laid eyes on Fat Fat, sitting on the couch naked, with her wrist and ankles bound with the phone cord.

"Bitch, come on in and sit down, why don't ya?" Trent said in a sinister tone from his hiding place in the far corner, then shoved Katasha to the couch. Once she was seated and scowling at him, he walked over and locked the door with his .44 Magnum tight in his grip.

"Trent, I swear we ain't got shit to do with this," Fat Fat cried as she tried to turn on the couch.

But Trent wasn't trying to hear shit as he walked over and slammed his fist in Katasha's eye, dazing her.

"Ah!" she wailed, then curled up on the floor.

He snatched the front room phone off the wall and started tying Katasha up with the cord. "Y'all hoes best get my shit back right fuckin' now!" Trent pointed the gun at Fat Fat, then at Katasha.

"What the hell you talkin' about? What shit? Please tell me what the fuck is going on!" Katasha screamed, scared as hell as she looked down the barrel of Trent's gun.

"Nikki stole dis nigga's car, girl! Can you believe that?" Fat Fat cried.

Trent drew back and slapped Katasha so hard that spit and a small stream of blood flew out of her mouth.

"Ow! What the…? Please don't do this, man. You heard my girl. It was Nikki, not us. We ain't have shit to do with your car, if that's what you're doin' all this fo'," Katasha said through sobs.

Trent raised the gun up again and put it right back in her face. "Naw, bitch, this ain't just about no damn car. This about a car with ten bricks and $10,000 cash in it, so y'all better get yer bitch on the phone and tell her to bring my shit back ASAP 'fo I put a cap in y'all ass. Trent growled as he swung and slapped Fat Fat with the gun, busting her lip.

"Ow! Oh God! Please, Trent! You know I'd never do no shit lie this to you," Fat Fat begged, leaning on Katasha, who was breathing hard and praying silently.

"All *that* was in your car? Oh no," Katasha said softly, realizing the situation was about to get really ugly—even worse than it already was. "Hold up. Just get me my purse," Katasha said.

Trent stopped pacing the room, walked over, and grabbed her bag that was lying by the door.

"Get my phone out," Katasha said. "Go to the contacts and hit Nikki's number."

Trent pressed the speed-dial number and then turned on the speaker button as the phone rang.

NIKKI

* * * * *

"Yeah?" I answered while pushing the customized Charger down the highway en route to Atlanta.

"Nikki, you gotta bring Trent's car back, girl!" Fat Fat yelled in the background.

Katasha chimed in, "Nikki, please! He gonna kill us if you don't bring his car back. No bullshit, Nikki. Please don't do this to us, li'l sis. Just bring his shit back," she pleaded.

Trent stood over both of them, listening in.

"Man, y'all tripping. That nigga ain't 'bout to kill y'all over no car. It ain't nothin' but more of y'all's bullshit, like the shit about your landlady sayin' too many people were staying there. Miss me wit' it, would ya? I may be young, but I ain't nowhere near dumb. Y'all told me to leave, so I'm gone," I said as I sped down the highway.

"Please, Nikki! He got dope and money in that car. It's way deeper than what you think. Please come back," Katasha pleaded as blood trickled down her chin.

"Bring my shit back, you little bitch. If you don't, you can kiss your folks goodbye, and I will hunt you down till I find you. You hold their lives and yours in your hands, so what are you gonna do?" Trent asked with a devious undertone in his voice.

I couldn't believe my luck. I had a car full of dope and money and was headed to the ATL. I smiled and thanked God for my good fortune. "Trent, I ain't scared of your trick ass! Thanks for the donation. Katasha and Fat Fat, y'all hoes hold it down. I'll catch up with y'all in traffic." With that, I pressed end on my cell and tossed it in the passenger seat.

* * * * *

Trent bit his bottom lip and threw the phone across the room, damn near shattering it on the wall. "Y'all hoes done fucked with the wrong nigga!" he raged through clenched teeth as he tightened his grip on the gun.

"Trent, you heard her! Like I told you, we ain't got nothin' to do wi—"

Pop! Pop!

Katasha took the two shots to her chest and face, unable to duck or dodge.

"Noooo! Trent, baby, come on! Please!" Fat Fat begged, shaking her head side to side violently before the single gunshot to the temple silenced her for good.

"Fuck-ass hoes," Trent spewed. He reached for his cell phone and realized that it, too, was gone. "Damn!" he said before he cracked the door open quietly, looked around to make sure the coast was clear, then eased out. He hurried to the corner store phone booth to call Mack.

CHAPTER 4

After finding out about the contents of the car, I took the next exit and pulled into a gas station. I searched the inside of the car and came up with nothing. When I opened the trunk, though, there was a big plastic bag in plain sight, secured with gray duct tape. I used the screwdriver sitting next to it to rip into it, and I smiled as I examined the contents of the package. Just like the girls had said, there were ten neatly wrapped bricks of cocaine. I searched the trunk further and found a leather case wedged between the spare tire and toolbox. When I opened it, I couldn't help cheesing; it was filled with crisp $100 bills, an even $10,000. I had drugs and money, enough to start a whole new life, and I knew the first thing I had to do was find a dope boy to help me turn the dope into cash.

It took fourteen hours to reach Atlanta, with a few pit-stops along the way. I was totally lost when I arrived in "The Black Mecca of the South." I exited at Peachtree Street and traveled south, through downtown Atlanta, looking for a hotel room.

The sky had went from dark back to light, and I still hadn't found a place to crash. Tired beyond belief, I got back on the interstate and headed east, in search of a Super 8 I'd seen advertised on a billboard. I took the exit onto Glenwood Road and followed it till I ended up in the motel parking lot. It was a slightly run-down place, but I didn't care. I was way past tired and hungry and was in desperate need of a bath.

At the counter in the front office, an Arab man quickly hung up his phone call when I approached the desk. "Hello. How may I help you?" he asked, focusing on my C-cups instead of my face.

"I need a room. How much?" I asked, thinking about the leather case in the car.

"I'll just need your ID and $49.95 a night," he said, putting his glasses on.

"ID?" I asked, hoping he'd let me slide.

"Yes. No room without proper ID," the man said in broken English.

"Man, come on! I lost my ID, and I'm tired as hell. Can't you help out?" I asked, giving him my best sad, sexy look.

Obviously, he had no interest in attending the pity party I'd invited him to, because he answered, "Sorry, ma'am. No ID, no room." Refusing to sympathize with me at all, he pointed at the sign on the wall that repeated the same policy.

I was tired and stinking, and the hotel desk clerk was pissing me off. This li'l old man was really pissing me off with this ID shit.

"This is some fuck shit straight up! Real bullshit! You funny-lookin' folks come over here and fuck shit up! Fuck you and this flea-bag hotel!" I screamed, knocking everything off of the front desk. "There're probably bedbugs and cum all

NIKKI

over the damn sheets anyway!"

The man's eyes widened in surprise. "Get out of me hotel now or me call the police, lady!" he screamed, turning around and grabbing the phone.

"Fuck you and the police!" I yelled, even though I knew I couldn't have the cops on my tail with all the contraband in the stolen car. I turned around and rushed out the door and somehow managed to bump right into the finest, sexiest nigga I'd ever seen.

"It's cool, Adunde. No need for the police," he said, holding his hand up to the desk clerk. "Damn, Miss Lady. Is it really that serious?" he asked, looking down at me with the sexiest eyes.

The man was all that and some. He had a fresh Caesar cut and a baby face with just enough roughness to make it known that he wasn't soft in no kind of way. He was sporting black True Religion jeans, a black Polo shirt, and a soft black letterman's jacket with an oversized "P" embroidered on it. The long diamond necklace and diamond studs in both of his ears put the icing on the cake, or at least I thought they did till I realized how bowlegged he was. He was so fine he could have been rapper Nas's younger brother.

"Serious?" I asked in disbelief, rolling my neck. "Yes, it's *that* serious! I'm tired, and need to freshen up!" I snapped not giving him any indication that I was digging his swag.

"You leave now, lady!" the Arab screamed as he picked up the items I'd knocked off the counter.

"Just chill, man. I got her." The sexy B-boy grabbed me by the arm and pulled me out the door. "Damn, shawty. You tryin'a go to jail over a damn room at the Super 8? What's up wit' you?" he asked in a Southern accent that only turned me on more.

I looked up into his eyes, fighting hard to keep my composure, not trying to show my crazy attraction. "His li'l bitch ass won't let me get a room just 'cause I ain't got no ID." I pouted, rolling my eyes and crossing my arms across my chest.

"Just calm down, pretty lady. I got you. What's your name anyway?" he asked, gazing at me.

The Southern drawl when he spoke the compliment made my heart flutter; the last and only other man who had ever called me "pretty" had been my father.

"I'm Nikki," I replied wondering where my sudden shyness was coming from.

"Nikki, I'm Prime. It's nice to meet you," he said, then extended his hand for a shake like a true gentleman.

"Nice to meet you too," I replied, gently shaking his smooth hand.

All I'd ever been taught about men was that I was supposed to play them and then move on to the next one. I'd never been taught how to be real when it came to the opposite sex. Looking at Prime, I wanted to see the other side of the game, the side where no one had any ulterior motives.

"We'll get you a room. What you doin' on this side of town this early in the morning anyway? I can tell by your accent that you ain't from around here," he said, scanning the parking lot like he was waiting for someone to show up.

I looked around the lot as well and then answered, "I'm from Chicago. I just got into town."

He looked at his watch, then up at the hotel entrance. "Chicago, huh? What brings you to The A?" he asked. When a burgundy Land Cruiser turned into the parking lot, he cut me off before I could feed him another lie. "Hold up right quick," he said, then waved the truck over to us. He stepped over to the truck, which was being driven buy a dark-skinned, very ugly Jamaican man with long, dusty braids and a mouthful of gold teeth.

I turned around like I wasn't listening to their conversation, making sure to take in every word.

"Yo, mon, we give you the whole motel to work, and you still ain't produced me money. You slackin', mon! You know why? *That's* why," the Jamaican spat, pointing at me.

I turned slightly, letting them know I'd heard him.

"Look, Rude Boy, that shit you dropped on me ain't no good, so all the fiends and the trap hustlers are taking their money out to Hooper Street. You need to change your supplier or somethin', 'cause this shit ain't gonna go, and I ain't about to take the blame for your bullshit product," Prime told him with aggravation in his tone.

"You sayin' me shit is no good?" Rude Boy growled.

"Yeah, man. That's what I'm tellin' you. The shit is…well, shit," Prime replied emphatically.

The Jamaican turned his face up, mugging Prime and gritting his teeth. "I'll be back at 5:00 for me money," he snapped.

"Fine. If this sorry-ass shit ain't moved by 5:00, I'll just give you back whatever I've got," Prime said, paying no mind to his facial expressions.

I had turned all the way around and was watching the exchange. I couldn't help digging the way Prime stood his ground and refused to back down from the man in the SUV.

"Give back? Ain't no givin' shit back! You just better have my money," Rude Boy snapped, then rolled the window up and pulled off.

Prime bit his bottom lip as he watched the truck speed out of the lot, tires squealing. "Fuck nigga!" he called out, then turned back to me.

"Excuse me?" I asked with raised brows.

"Nothing. Just follow me." He snatched open the door of his customized Ford F-250 and climbed in behind the wheel.

I got in the Challenger and followed him out of the lot. As we weaved in and out of traffic, I smiled. I'd already found my dope boy to move all of Trent's shit in the trunk. For once, my luck seemed to be turning around.

CHAPTER 5

"We ain't gon' wait on you all day. Niggas ready to hit the block," Greedy told Trent as he and his young crew waited to pick up the drop he'd already paid Trent for.

Trent and Coon had ridden around all night, trying to find his Challenger in the city. Meanwhile, in Atlanta, I'd cut off my cell when it started blowing up with unfamiliar numbers.

"I'll meet you at 6:00 down at Roscoe's BBQ," Trent told Greedy as Coon ran his hand over his bald head. He knew if they didn't get Greedy's dope or money, there was going to be trouble.

"Man, we gotta meet before that, 'cause I got folks waiting to spend now. I'll just come to where you at," Greedy suggested, eager to get his hands on the four blocks he'd already paid for.

Trent had put Greedy and two more drops on hold while he was out at Fat Fat's spot tricking off, and now he didn't have their dope or money. "We outside the city right now, handlin' some other shit, but we'll be back around 3:00. Just be down there at 3:30," he lied, hoping he'd locate his car by then.

"A'ight. That'll work," Greedy said before ending the call.

"Man, where this bitch at?" Coon yelled as he drove back out to the south side of Chicago.

Trent loaded his Glock as they made another round through the city. "This bitch gonna pay, my nigga, straight up," he seethed, looking out at the passing cars and hoping to spot his.

"Greedy and them gonna want their shit, bro. How in the hell you let the bitch take your car anyway? How we gon' play this shit if we can't find the scandalous li'l ho?" Coon asked, pulling back out into the main road.

"Man, just hit another block," Trent said, ignoring the question and growing more and more frustrated by the minute.

"This bitch ain't nowhere to be found, bruh," Coon said, turning back around in a gas station parking lot.

"Fuck! I can't believe this shit!" Trent punched the dashboard of the Cadillac, drawing a hateful look from Coon.

"Man, be careful with my car, nigga!"

Coon pushed the Cadillac through the neighborhood for the third time, and they rode in silence for a while. After riding through the back streets again with no luck, they finally gave up.

"Just head out to Roscoe's. I'll have to let Greedy know what time it is," Trent said, pulling out his cell phone.

Coon took a deep breath and readied himself to deal with Greedy, the notorious street goon who was known for his crazy crew and treacherous ways.

"Hello?" Greedy answered, looking at his watch and grimacing when he saw that it was only 2:30.

"Say, bro, we on our way to Roscoe's now," Trent said. He hoped things wouldn't get out of hand when he broke the bad news to Greedy.

"A'ight. I'm on my way." Greedy got up from the kitchen table where he and his crew had been busy loading their high-powered weapons, staying on point just in case shit popped off in the street.

Greedy's crew had the entire south side of Chicago on lock. He wasn't the average dealer. If he couldn't beat out the competition with his prices, he sent his young crew to eliminate them. They were well known throughout the city for their crazy, deadly ways, and no one wanted to go to war with them.

Twenty minutes later, Greedy and his crew were pulling up in Roscoe's parking lot in their tinted-window, old-school Chevy Impala. Trent and Coon were in their car in front of Roscoe's waiting on them. Seeing Greedy pull into the lot, Trent stepped out of the car and made himself seen. Greedy parked on the far side of the lot, exited the car, and walked over to meet them.

"What it do?" Trent said, giving Greedy some dap as he climbed back into the front passenger seat.

Greedy opened the back door and got in. "What we lookin' like? Time to get this show on the road, don't you think?" Greedy said, rubbing his hands together.

Trent looked over at Coon, who was nervously tapping the steering wheel. He took a deep breath before he spoke. "Yo, fam' I ain't gonna beat around the bush wit' cha. I got hit for the work and need a li'l time to get your money back or the work. Just give me a week to straighten this shit out," Trent said, slowly easing his hand to the gun resting in his lap.

"Nigga, what'd you just say? I know I ain't heard you right. Say that shit again," Greedy snapped, raising from the back seat and leaning his head over the front seat.

"Straight up, bruh, I got hit for my whole play. No bullshit. I got some shit in the mix though. Just give me a li'l time to get this shit in motion," Trent asked again, refusing to look Greedy in his beady bug eyes.

"We just need a li'l bit, fam'," Coon added, looking across the lot at Greedy's crew in the Chevy. They were passing a blunt around, waiting on their boss to return with the dope.

Greedy cut his eyes downward and peeped Trent's gun. Inwardly fuming, he sat back and held his tongue. For the moment, in their car, he was outnumbered and outgunned. "Man, this some fuck shit, but it is what it is. How much time y'all need?" he asked feeling like he'd been tried and disrespected at the same time.

"Just a week. My word, you'll have your shit or your money back by then," Trent answered, relieved that Greedy was being somewhat understanding.

"A'ight. One week. Just hit me then," Greedy said. He then pushed the car door open and stepped out with a frown on his face.

Buzz! Buzz!

Trent reached down to answer his vibrating cell phone. Just as he was putting it to his ear, shots rang out. When he looked up, all he saw was Greedy and his crew busting shots from high-powered guns.

Tat! Boom! Pop! Tat! Tat! Boom! Pop! Pop! It sounded like the Fourth of July had broken loose right there in Roscoe's parking lot.

"Go! Go! Step on that shit!" Trent screamed at Coon, dropping his phone. He heard the engine revving, but the car wasn't moving.

Coon had been killed instantly by a shot to the head, and his right foot was stuck on the gas pedal, pushing it to the floor. Trent ducked and dodged in the front seat as the bullets tore through the automobile, many of them smashing into the already dead driver. By the time the volley of bullets stopped, Trent had been hit once in the face and twice in the side. Greedy and his goons jumped back in the Chevy and rushed out of the lot, squealing tires all the way.

Seconds later, sirens were rushing to the scene. Coon was dead, and Trent had blacked out.

When he woke up in the hospital that night, he couldn't believe he'd survived the attack, only losing his right eye in the process. As he lay back in bed, all he could think about was the person responsible for it all.

CHAPTER 6

We pulled into the Holiday Inn parking lot, which made the previous motel look like a junkyard. I pulled up and parked next to his truck.

"I'll get you a room," he said, and he stepped out of his truck and entered the hotel lobby.

I could tell he was pissed off because of the Jamaican man in the truck, but I was glad he was still willing to help me out.

A few minutes later, he was back with my room key.

"Thanks," I said, then followed him around to the front side of the hotel.

When we parked and got out, he tried his best to hide his wandering eyes but failed miserably. "Let me help you with your bag," he said, then walked back to the trunk of the car.

There wasn't anything in the trunk but ten kilos and $10,000, and I wasn't ready to bring him into my business just yet. I was eager to get rid of the dope, but I had to be sure he could be trusted. "I've only got that one bag in the back seat. Thanks for helping me out though," I said. I glanced at the number on the room key, then looked up at the numbers on the doors.

"Down there on the left," he said, as if he frequented the hotel a lot.

"You must be out here all the time. Damn, you doing it like that?" I asked playfully, even though I was really dead serious.

"Born and raised around here. Been runnin' 'round these parts since I was a jit. This the spot where I lay my head when I'm too tired to head back across town to my spot. The other spot we just left was my get-money spot," he explained as we walked, side by side, up to the room.

"Get-money spot? What you do to get money?" I asked, pretending I was curious, since I already knew damn well what he did for a living.

He looked at me and smiled, revealing his single dimple and perfect pearly whites. That look had me wanting to strip him naked and give him the business. Instead, I somehow kept my composure and smiled back.

"I sell insurance," he answered sarcastically; it was clear he knew I already had him figured out.

"What kind of insurance?" I shot back, challenging his lie.

"Hmm. All these questions about me. Why don't you tell me a li'l something about you?"

"Like what?"

"Like…how long you gonna be here? And where your man at?" he asked as we reached the room.

I inserted the key and stepped into the nice, comfortable, cozy room.

He followed me in and closed the door behind him.

"That depends. I haven't decided yet. And as for a man, I ain't got one," I said as I turned to face him.

"What it depend on? And why the hell you ain't got no

man? How old are you anyway?" he asked, catching me off guard.

I paused before I answered. "How long I stay is gonna depend on whether or not I find anything worth stayin' for. I ain't got no man because all y'all do is play games. And, as for my age…well, a real woman never tells," I replied hoping he wouldn't push for a more direct answer.

I had made my mind up off the top that I was going to bag this fine-ass nigga, and I wasn't about to fall short on that. I kept telling myself it was only about him moving the dope, but with every passing minute and every word he said, I kept finding myself digging him on another level.

"I hear ya," he said and didn't press any further.

"Can I ask you something?" I asked as I jumped up on the bed and pulled my shoes off.

"Yeah. What up?" he said, leaning back on the wall and crossing his strong arms.

"What was that all about back at the hotel?" I asked while pulling my socks off.

"Well, I didn't want that Arab-ass desk clerk callin' the cops because…well, for one, the spot would be hot, and no money could be made for hours. For another thing, I didn't wanna see them hauling your sexy little ass off to jail in handcuffs," he said emphatically.

"No, not that part. I understand about the police. Who in the hell ever wants them involved in anything? I meant the man in the truck. What was up with him?" I looked up into his eyes and could tell they had seen a lot in his years. I could tell he'd been there and done that by the way he carried himself. I could also tell he'd played his share of games as well, that he'd fooled many with his good looks and calm demeanor. The one thing I was sure of, though, was that he wasn't caked up like he put on, especially if he was working for someone else. I quickly came to the conclusion that Prime was a trap nigga with boss potential.

"Oh…that. Nigga sold me some bad shit and is lookin' for me to pay him for it," he said, as if I would buy the lie.

"Huh? If he sold you that shit, how he gon' be pulling up demanding payment for what you already bought? You gotta pay for it twice? That don't make no sense. It sounds to me like he fronted you some dope, and now he's looking for his money. You work for him, right?" I said, trying to purposely make him feel like a chump.

He frowned and stood up off the wall. "Work for him? Damn, shawty, I don't work for nobody but myself. I'm a made nigga for real," he said with a hint of attitude.

I laughed to myself at his sudden change of attitude; I'd just stepped on his overinflated ego. "Oh. My bad. I must have heard you two wrong. I just thought—"

He quickly cut me off. "Yeah, well, you thought wrong! I gotta be getting back out to the spot. I'll come back through and holla at ya later." He was obviously upset and embarrassed.

He left without asking me for my number or giving me his. I knew then that I'd effectively poured gas on his already burning fire, and he was pissed. I just let him walk out without even saying a word, as if I didn't care one way or the other. I had to play the game, too, because there was no way I was going to let Prime know I was thirsty for him, even if I actually was.

I planned to take a quick nap then get up, eat, and head to the mall. As soon as he closed the door, I lay back on the bed. Minutes later, I was fast asleep, tired as hell.

* * * * *

Prime parked his truck behind the hotel, tucked his 9mm in his waistband, and walked over to the room he sold dope out of. The motel was a known drug spot, and most of the rooms were occupied by junkies and prostitutes. Undercover drug users like school teachers, cops, and even church deacons would cruise through in search of a daily fix of drugs and sex.

Prime had risen through the ranks of Rude Boy's organization rather quickly. He'd started off small, just selling $100 slabs. When he moved those with ease, Rude Boy upped his package to half a kilo and put him in charge over a couple of his drug spots. Prime settled in the Old English Motel and locked it down, and all his years of hustling in the trap had paid off. Rube Boy was part-owner of the hotel. As soon as he'd discovered that a young Arab by the name of Adunde had bought the place, he'd sent a few of his crewmembers to terrorize all the tenants until no one dared to rent a room there, so the place was always vacant, and the Arab was losing money left and right just to keep his newly acquired hotel open. Just as Adunde was about to throw in the towel, Rude Boy stepped in and offered his assistance to keep trouble away, in exchange for part ownership. The Arab saw a chance to salvage his bad investment and agreed. Now every room was occupied, and the place brought in more and more money every day. Adunde was relatively happy, and Rude Boy had access to a prime drug spot. A couple of outsiders had tried to slide through from time to time to sell their dope, but they were always quickly run off by Banta Man, one of Rude Boy's enforcers who would kill at a nod of Rude Boy's dreadlocked head.

Prime had quickly become the go-to man in the hotel, and it

GEORGE SHERMAN HUDSON

didn't take time for him to start picking up clientele from other parts of the city. He was quickly making a name for himself, and that was why he refused to sell bad dope that would most definitely scar his reputation. Rude Boy had fronted him a kilo of bad dope that not even the smoked-out crack-heads wanted, and the stuff wasn't moving at all.

He walked to the bed, flipped the mattress over, and pulled out the stash Rude Boy had given to him, still in the bag. He shook his head, looking down at the dope he refused to put off on his loyal customers. He took a seat at the table and tried to think of what his next move should be.

A few minutes later, Prime nodded off, tired from being up all night, moving what little he could of the bad product.

A few hours later, the room door slammed into the wall, waking him up.

Bam!

"What the fuck?" he screamed, jumping up.

"Yo, mon, I'm here to collect," Rude Boy said, standing in the middle of the room with Banta Man. He tucked the extra key from the front desk in his pocket.

Prime looked from him to Banta Man, a giant holding a gym bag. Banta Man stood well over six feet tall and weighed close to 300 pounds. He sported the same dusty, dirty dreads as Rude Boy, and his partially covered his acne-scarred face. He never smiled, but his frown always gave a clear view dull gold teeth, stained from years of inhaling cigarette and weed smoke.

"Um—" Prime started.

"Get my money, and I'll have more product for you," Rude Boy said. He glanced back at Banta Man and nodded toward the gym bag with two more kilos of bad dope.

If Prime would have known from the beginning that Rude Boy was trying to push all the bad shipment he'd been tricked with on his first buy from a new connect, he would have refused it from the start. Rude boy had been sold twenty-five kilos of bad dope, and the seller's phone number had suddenly been disconnected. Now he was pushing it all on his workers to get rid of it, including Prime. Everyone who had been given the work had the same gripe, saying it was no good, but Rude Boy didn't care. He just wanted his money.

"Rude Boy, I told you what the biz is with that shit. It's bad, and they ain't buying it." Prime lifted off the bed, grabbed the bag he had pulled from under the mattress, and held it out to him.

Rude Boy looked at him with fire in his eyes.

Banta Man picked on his boss's rage, so he set the bag down on the table and slowly eased his hand over the blade he carried in his waistband.

Prime didn't flinch; he was fed up with Rude Boy pushing him around like he was a sucker.

"After all I do for you, mon, you just gon' hand my shit back?" Rude Boy asked, bringing a frown to Prime's face.

Prime looked at him like he was crazy. Since Rude Boy didn't seem to understand what he'd told him, he said it again. "Fam', you know I'm down with the movement, but this here ain't gonna sell at all. The shit just ain't no good, and even the lowlifes on the street know the difference," he said again.

This time, Rude Boy flew off into a rage. He thought about the other seventeen kilos that sat in his storage unit and snapped, "Fuck you, mon!" He then swung and hit Prime unexpectedly in the nose, knocking him back on the bed.

"Ow!" Prime cried, trying to stop the gushing blood with

his hand. "What the fuck!?"

By the time he started to lift up to do something about it, Banta Man was on him with the eight-inch blade to his throat.

"Move, mon!" Rude Boy told Banta Man as he stood over Prime with his gun in his grip.

"C'mon, Rude Boy. What the fuck is this all about, man?" Prime asked as blood continued pouring from his nose.

Rude Boy smiled widely, showing all of his gold teeth, then drew back with his gun tight in his big hands and started beating and pistol-whipping the shit out of Prime. By the time he stepped away from the bed, Prime was all swollen and bloody. "Get me money." Rude Boy grabbed the bag off the floor and threw it on the bed next to Prime, letting him know he expected him to get off the other as well, and then he and Banta Man turned and exited the room.

Prime made his way slowly off the bed. Aching, bruised, and bleeding, he stumbled through the room in an incoherent daze. He held his head as he tried to make it to the door, but he passed out before he could grip the handle.

CHAPTER 7

Knock! Knock!
    "Housekeeping!" screamed the housekeeper from the other side of the door.

I couldn't believe I had slept all night long without waking up once. "Damn," I said groggily as I rolled out of bed. "No thank you!" I shouted to the maid.

I was starving and badly in need of a freshening up. As soon as I heard her walk down the hall, I jumped up, took a quick shower, and slid into a pair of jeans and t-shirt. I had planned to hit the mall the night before to buy a couple of new outfits, some underwear, and other necessities, but the sandman had taken over, so I had no choice but to wear the old clothes I'd brought with me.

All of a sudden, it hit me that Prime hadn't come back to check on me like he'd promised. I knew I'd made him mad, but I didn't think it was all that serious. I had ten kilos in my trunk, and I needed him to help me get off it. I looked at the time and knew housekeeping would be circling back around any minute, so I grabbed the room key, got in the car, and headed to the front office to turn it in.

The young boy wasn't behind the counter this time, but I told the woman behind the desk, "Hi. I wanna return this key."

She looked up from the computer she was typing on and reached out to take the key. Before she grabbed it, it hit me. "Actually, maybe I should stay another night. I think I'll be able to convince my fiancé. Your city is lovely." I crossed my fingers, hoping I wouldn't have to go through the checkout process.

"Okay. No problem. Just give me a second. What room was it?" she asked as she kept keying information into the computer.

I looked down at the key for the room number and told it to her, hoping no ID would be necessary; the last thing I needed was a repeat of what had happened with Adunde.

"That'll be $69.95. Will that be cash or credit?" she asked, looking over the rim of her glasses.

"Cash," I said, then dug out one of the $100 bills I'd taken out of the case.

It took the old lady five minutes to complete the transaction. "All right. Here you go. Have a nice day," she said with a motherly smile that reminded me of my Aunt Mattie.

"Thanks. Can you tell me where the nearest mall is?"

"The closest is South DeKalb Mall, about ten minutes up the road. Go right up to the light, make a right, and keep going all the way out till you see it. You can't miss it," she said, using her finger to point in the direction.

"I'll just put it in my GPS. South DeKalb, you said?" I asked.

"Yes. That's South D-e-K-a-l-b," she spelled it out, as if I was slow.

"Uh...thanks," I said, giving her a crooked smile before I left the lobby.

I topped the hill and made a left as the GPS instructed, then drove all the way out until I saw the mall. I circled the parking lot twice before a found a close enough spot; I wasn't about to park the car in the back where it might be stolen. A DeKalb County police car cruised by slowly as I got out of the car. I knew that every time I got behind the wheel of the stolen vehicle, an unlicensed driver with drugs and drug money in the trunk, I was taking a big risk. I didn't know if Trent had reported the theft yet or not, but just to be safe, I'd already made plans to find something else to drive so I could dump the Challenger. I walked around, popped the trunk, and opened the case. I pulled out $700 and stuffed the large bills in my front pants pocket, then went inside and did a little shopping trip for a couple of new outfits, some hygiene products, underwear, and a couple pair of sneakers.

"Thanks...and have a nice day," said the cashier at the Chic-fil-A in the food court said as she handed me my chicken sandwich and waffle fries.

I grabbed my bag off the counter, ready to dig in.

"Damn, li'l shawty. You need some help carrying them bags?" an old has-been said as he walked up to me. He was dressed like he thought he was still a teenager, in a two-sizes-too-big throwback jersey and baggy sweats.

I looked him up and down, then walked around him. "I appreciate the offer, but I'm good," I said, speeding up my pace when he made it clear that he was trying to follow me.

"Yeah, you good, girl, but you could be better though," he said, trying to catch up.

"I'm not interested," I finally snapped, rolling my eyes.

"Fuck you den, bitch. It's yo' loss," he called out as I pushed through the doors exiting the mall.

"Fuck you too," I mumbled, then quickly made my way across the lot to the car.

All that was on my mind was getting settled into the new city. I got in the car and put the name of the raggedy motel that he sold drugs out of into the GPS. Since Prime wasn't going to come back to me, I was going to go to him. I followed the directions to the motel and saw his truck sitting in front of Room 12, so I pulled up next to it and got out.

Knock! Knock!

When I didn't get an answer, I knocked again, harder this time, just in case he was sleep. At first, I hadn't considered that he might be getting his groove on, but when that thought hit me, I turned to leave. Just as I was turning, I noticed a small part in the window curtain, and I walked over and peeked in out of sheer curiosity. My heart dropped when I looked in and saw Prime sprawled out on the floor, with blood soaking the carpet around him.

I grabbed the doorknob and tried it; to my surprise, it opened. I rushed into the room and ran over to him, only to find that he was barely breathing. "Prime? Prime!" I yelled as I knelt over him lost at what to do.

I grabbed the phone from the nightstand and started to dial 911, but before I pressed the last digit, I realized it was probably a stupid move. There was too much dope in the car I'd taken from Trent, and there was no telling what illegal substances or weapons Prime had in the room. I ran in the bathroom and dampened two towels, then ran back over to him. He stirred as I placed the warm towel over his face and head.

"Aw…" He groaned as his eyes flicked open.

"You okay? What happened?" I asked, removing the first towel replacing it with the second.

"Oh, man. Damn…" He moaned in pain as he tried to sit up.

I could tell he'd been out cold all night, because he was still wearing the same clothes from the day before. "We need to get you to the hospital," I suggested.

He sat up in the middle of the floor, holding the towel on his head. "Nah, I'm good. I just need to get up outta here," he said, then tried to stand.

"You sure you can drive?" I asked, helping him to his feet.

"Yeah. I'm a'ight. Grab my gun outta the draw, and get them two bags." He slowly made his way to the door.

I did as I was told, then followed him out to the parking lot. "You sure you're all right?" I asked, pulling his truck door open for him.

"Yeah," he replied. With several more pained groans, he pulled himself up into the truck and fished his keys from his pocket.

I handed him the bags and gun, gazing up at his swollen baby face, all bruised and broken. "Look, why don't you just come back to my room for a while, till you can pull yourself together? I need to talk to you about something anyway," I said.

He didn't put up much of a fight. "All right," he said. "I'll follow you back around to your room."

I turned and walked to the Challenger. As I drove to my motel room, I kept my eyes on him in the rearview mirror as he followed me. We both parked in front of my room, and I helped him out of his truck.

"Come on in so we can get you together," I said, surprisi even myself that I was so genuinely concerned about a

I didn't even really know. That wasn't my style at all. I kept telling myself I was doing it because I needed his assistance with the ten kilos I had to unload in a hurry, but I knew there was something deeper to it than that. The truth was, I was really feeling Prime. "Just lie there for a minute. I got you. What the hell happened to you anyway? Does this got anything to do with that man you owe?" I asked.

He sat on the bed with his head down. "I'ma kill that fuck nigga," he mumbled, looking down at the floor.

"Can't go doin' no crazy shit, man. You gotta stay cool," I said. I didn't want him to do anything stupid that might kill my chances of getting him to help me, so I'd already made up my mind to let him in on my dirty little secret.

"Nah, shawty, I ain't 'bout to let no nigga play me off the street. I'll handle his ass though," he said, balling his fist up.

"You ain't workin' for him no more? Er...I mean, wit' him?" I corrected myself, remembering his words. The last thing I needed was for him to get angry and storm out again, though he couldn't have moved as fast in his current condition as he had the day before.

"Fuck that nigga. That's over wit. I'm gonna get off this bad shit and keep everything I make off it. When I see that nigga, I'm gonna let him know it is what it is," he said in a real tough-guy tone that I liked.

"So that's what's in the bags, bad stuff?"

"Bags of shit. Not even the crack-heads want it. Damn, I'd be lucky if I could give it away to a fuckin' alley cat."

"What if you had some good stuff?"

"What you mean?"

"I mean, if you had something other than that bad shit, could you sell it...and fast?"

He slowly stood up and walked over to the bathroom mirror, then looked at the reflection of his swollen, bruised face. He frowned. "Man!" he growled, turning his face from side to side to get a better look.

"It ain't that bad. You still handsome," I said, looking over his shoulder.

"Thanks, but to answer your question, yeah, if I had good shit, it wouldn't be a problem to move it. Fuckin' around with this bad shit is making shit ten times harder. I'm just gonna drop it off on my li'l young niggas for the low tomorrow," he said as he walked back over to sit on the bed. "Why you so interested in work all of a sudden?" he asked, looking at me quizzically.

"Can I trust you?" I asked bluntly.

He gave me a strange look, then answered, "Yeah. Why?"

I walked over and sat next to him on the bed. "Just wanted to know," I said with a smile. "How much you make off a kilo?" I asked, knowing it was a nice amount not about to be played short.

"That depends on how it's sold. Whole, you can get about $32,000 to $36,000, but if it's broke down, you'll get about fifty grand off it. Why? You trying to be a dope girl or somethin'? Shit. Maybe I oughtta be askin' if I can trust you, 'cause I'm telling you a li'l too much," he said, turning to look at me.

"Yes, you can trust me, and yes, I'm trying to get in the game. Can you help me or not?" I asked, looking into his eyes pleadingly.

He let out a light laugh and returned my gaze. "In the game, huh? What, exactly, are you trying to do?"

I could tell by his tone that he wasn't taking me seriously, and it was starting to piss me off. "If could get you good dope, maybe you could sell it, and we could split the money."

"You can get good dope, huh?" he said, stifling a laugh, as if he didn't believe me.

"Let's say I get a kilo. You could get $20,000 for me, and you keep the rest," I suggested.

"Shit, I can do better than that. I'll get you $25,000 for it, 'cause it's gonna cost you at least twenty grand, unless you got a hell of a connect," he answered with curiosity in his tone.

"When can you be ready?" I asked, knowing I'd caught him off guard.

"Uh…well, I ain't about no games right now," he snapped, getting serious as he gently ran his hand over his swollen face.

"This ain't no game, Prime, no bullshit. I'm dead serious," I replied.

"A'ight. Then I'm ready now. What's up, baby girl?" he said, obviously trying to call my bluff, even though I wasn't bluffing.

"I can trust you right?" I asked again, firmer this time.

"I already answered that," he said with attitude. "Look, I don't know what you're up to, but fuck it. I knew you was bullshittin'."

"I ain't bullshitting. I got you, but you best calm the fuck down and listen."

"All right. Go on."

"It's a long story. First off, I don't have family here. I'm here because I stole my friend's boyfriend's car and drove here. My parents were killed when I was a child, and I ain't got nobody, so when times got hard in the Chi, I decided to move South, since I hear the living is cheaper down here. Long story short, I stole that car and ran down here to start a new life," I said.

He listened carefully to my half-truths, surprised by my

revelations. "Um, nice story and all, but what's all that got to do with any dope? Where does that come in at?" he asked with a confused look on his face.

"There were ten kilos in the car. I didn't know it was there, but it is, and—"

His eyes grew big, and he cut me off. "Ten bricks! Where they at?" he asked excitedly, which made me put my guard up higher.

"I hid them," I lied, thinking about the bag of dope in the trunk. "I'm sure it's good stuff though—at least better than the bad stuff your Jamaican friend gave you."

"That nigga ain't nobody's friend. But anyway, you help me, and I'll help you. You see what I'm dealing with, but with that much blow, we can get all the way straight," he said, now ready to make it happen.

"Okay. I'm down with that. Just gimme a minute. I'll be right back."

I got in the car, drove to the back of the hotel, and parked. I needed time to map everything out and to hide the money. After looking around to make sure no one was watching, I took out the leather case and tucked it into the bags with my earlier mall purchases, then made my way back around to the room. I tapped the horn when I pulled up.

He came out the door to the car.

"It's in the back," I said, popping the trunk from the inside.

By the time I was out of the car, Prime had the bags in hand and was heading back to the room. Inside, he took out each plastic-wrapped package and inspected it. He tore the plastic back on one of them and looked at it closer. After making sure they were all legit, he placed them back in the bag. "This is some good shit. It'll be gone in no time," he said, the look on his face letting me know he was feeling good about our business deal.

"Just don't run off on me," I said playfully, even though I really meant it.

He frowned as if I'd insulted him in the worst way. "Not in my blood. I'm a real nigga, uncut. I got you," he said, then grabbed his keys from the table.

"You leavin' already?" I asked, looking into his battered face. "You still all bruised and shit."

"Yeah, I gotta get to the house, shower, and change. Hold all this down. I won't be gone long," he said.

I followed him out to his truck.

He opened his truck door grabbed his gun and the other two bags of dope. "Hold all this shit down, too, and don't open the door for nobody. You know how to use that piece?" he asked, nodding toward the weapon as he handed it to me.

I gripped the gun tightly. "Just cock and shoot, right?" I asked, recalling the shows I'd seen on TV.

"Yeah. I'll be back. Stay inside and keep the door locked for anyone but me." He picked up his phone from the passenger seat and looked at it. "Fuck!" he said as he read his missed texts, then looked back at me. "What's your number?" he asked, obviously still bothered about something.

I called out my number.

He quickly stored it in his phone, brought the truck engine to life, and pulled out of the parking lot.

Then, just like I was told, I hurried back into the room and locked the door behind me.

CHAPTER 8

A couple hours after securing all the dope and the gun, I stepped out, grabbed my bags from the car, and took a long, hot bath. I couldn't shake my thoughts of Prime. I washed my hair, pulled it back in a ponytail, and slipped into my new D&G jeans and shirt.

After my bath, I walked over to the table and looked at Prime's gun. I picked it up, checked it out closely, then laid it back on the table next to the dope. I then curiously pulled out one of the kilos. How can this block of shit be worth so much money? Ruin so many lives? Shaking my head, I stuck the cocaine back in the bag and sat down in the chair.

Knock! Knock!

The hard banging on the door scared me. I jumped up, peeked out the peephole, and was relieved to see that it was only Prime on the other side. I unlatched the chainlock to let him in. My mouth hit the floor as I looked him up and down. Despite his slightly swollen and bruised face, he was still fine as hell. He was Polo from head to toe and smelling good, and

I noticed a small black bag in his hand. "You made it back this time," I said, stepping to the side letting him in.

"Yeah, just in time to get to the money," he said, crossing the room to the table. "Has anybody ever told you that you favor actress Lauren London?" he asked, setting the small bag on the table.

"Um, no, but I guess that's a good thang, right?" I asked, sliding the chainlock closed.

"Yeah. She's sexy as hell," he said, unzipping the small bag.

It surprised me that he hadn't really made a move on me since we'd met. I could tell by his subtle compliments and comments that he found me attractive, so I couldn't understand why he hadn't tried to get some like most men already would have. The fact that he hadn't come on to me only made me want him that much more.

"So…what's next?" I asked, watching him pull the dope out of the bag.

"Since this good is so potent, I'ma use it to fix this bad and get off all this shit at once. I'll have your $250,000 in no time. All you gotta do is sit back and be cute while I handle all the business."

Like an expert, he carefully opened all the packages, then pulled out the digital scale, plastic bags, and tape he'd brought with him. I watched as he mixed the drugs I'd given him with the bad stuff he had, breaking it all down into a fine powder. He then took portions of it, weighed it, and filled the bags, careful not to spill any of it. After he finished, he pulled out his cell and started making calls and setting up deliveries.

"I gotta make these runs now. I'll be back in a couple of hours," he said, putting all the little bags of mixed dope in one big bag.

"Can I ride with you? I'm tired of sitting around this room. You said you was gonna teach me the game anyway. What better way for me to learn then hands on?" I said, then started putting on my shoes, not about to take no for an answer.

"You don't need—" he started.

"So you're not gonna teach me?" I asked, frowning at him. "Not even after I gave you the drugs?"

He blew air out and looked at me. "A'ight, fine. Come on," he told me reluctantly, grabbing the bag of dope and his gun.

We climbed in his truck, hit the main road, and darted out into traffic, heading to the first business deal meeting spot. Ten minutes later, we were pulling into the Church's Chicken parking lot.

Tap! Tap!

A big black brother tapping on the extended cab door scared me, making me jump. He pulled the back door open and climbed in.

"What up, Big? I see you got it poppin' out here. Here's ya order," Prime said, handing the man eighteen grams of the packaged powder.

Big looked at me as he passed Prime a wad of bills.

Prime made small talk while counting the money.

"I should be back at you in no time," the man said, again cutting his eyes at me.

"I got whatever you need. Be safe and just get at me when you ready," Prime said as he passed me the $18,000 he'd just made.

After giving Prime some dap, Big hopped out of the car.

Prime dropped the truck into drive and headed to the next drop-off location.

"So it's that easy, huh?" I asked, dividing the money and

tucking some in each of my pockets.

"It is when you got clientele like mines," Prime joked. He held up his phone to show me his contact list.

Two hours later, we were holding over $100,000, and his phone was still ringing off the hook. Night had fallen, though, so Prime told his last two calls he'd get with them the next day; he refused to do business after dark.

Beep! Beep!

As we sat at a red light on Memorial Drive on our way back to the room, a car horn blared.

I looked down at the car, then over to Prime, who looked like a deer caught in headlights.

"So that's how it is! This is why you ain't been home at night, nigga! Man, fuck you!" a dark-skinned, exotic-looking chick called out the window of a plum-colored BMW 3 Series.

Prime sat up in his seat and was about to respond, but she wasn't hearing it. Her tires screeched as the light turned green.

I cut my eyes over at Prime and could tell he was sincerely bothered and upset that the woman was tripping on him. "Sorry. Hope I didn't get you in trouble." It suddenly made sense why he hadn't tried to push up on me; he already had a woman.

"Nah, I'm straight," he said as his phone started lighting up, alerting him of a call or text. He picked up the phone, read the text, then slammed the phone on the console.

"You sure you all right?" I asked again as he broke the speed limit down the main street on the way back to the hotel.

"I'm fine!" he snapped, whipping the truck into the lot. "Count out $75,000 and leave the rest. We'll get back on the grind tomorrow," he told me, rushing me out of the truck.

I was somewhat hurt by his rudeness, but he clearly wanted

to get back to the woman who held his heart. Besides, the money made me feel a little better. I really wanted to question him about the woman, but I dismissed the thought. I knew it wasn't my place; besides, our deal was supposed to be about the money—or at least that was what I wanted to believe. "Okay…uh, talk to you later," I said as I climbed out.

He didn't even tell me goodbye as he sped out of the lot to see about his pissed-off woman.

CHAPTER 9

"I'm not puttin' up with this shit, Prime! I can't believe you! I can't do this no more," Taj cried as she rushed through the apartment they shared, hurriedly and messily packing her bags.

"Hold up, Taj! Just chill the fuck out, would ya? Ain't shit goin' on with that girl but business, baby! Please just sit down and hear me out," Prime begged as he walked behind Taj his high school sweetheart and fiancé.

"Yeah, whatever, Prime. She's just like the last bitch I caught you with! You can have your li'l hoes, 'cause I'm done!" she screamed, then ran in the bathroom and locked the door behind her.

Beep! Beep!

Prime stopped and looked down at the unfamiliar number on his phone. "Yeah?" he screamed angrily into it.

"Yo, mon, I'll be there tomorrow for some of me money," Rude Boy said casually, as if the beating had never happened.

"Nigga, fuck you and yo' money! I ain't got shit for you but these hollow-points when I catch up wit' you! Quit hittin' my shit up. I'll see you in the street!" Prime was mad and didn't give a fuck about anything but Taj; the love of his life was about to walk out on him because of his new business partner, and he couldn't have cared less about Rude Boy's threats.

"Fuck me? No, fuck *you,* mon! I'm gonna skin you alive, boy!" Rude Boy said menacingly, then clicked off the line.

Prime tossed his phone on the bed as Taj stormed out of the bathroom, still in tears. "Taj, baby, please just stop and hear me out! I swear it ain't shit with that girl. I just stopped her from blowing up the spot, then helped her get a room. It's nothing else!" Prime explained as Taj snatched her car keys off the computer desk.

"You think I'm stupid or some shit, Prime? Why you ridin' 'round wit' her then?" Taj yelled, rushing by him.

Prime jumped in front of her, desperate to stop her from leaving. "Taj, you gonna listen to me now!" he yelled, reaching down to grab her keys out of her trembling hand.

Prime and Taj had been together since high school. They were first loves and had been eagerly looking forward to tying the knot the following summer. Taj was the complete opposite of Prime, an elementary school teacher to his street hustler; Paula Abdul's words rang true, because the fact that they were so very different did make them all that more attractive to each other. Taj was constantly on Prime's case, however, wanting him to leave the streets alone, but he knew working a 9:00-to-5:00 wouldn't allow him to afford the lifestyle he wanted for them. The couple had been through a lot together, and more than once, they'd almost broken up over the many hoochies who were constantly trying to bed the handsome up-and-coming hustler. Prime had only given in once, and Taj had reluctantly forgiven. She'd never forgotten, though, and she swore if he did it again, she would leave him. Since then, Prime had been absolutely loyal to Taj, and he was excited to give her his last name. He refused to let the love of his life walk out the door when he hadn't done anything wrong to deserve it.

"Get outta my way and give me my keys, Prime! I ain't playing wit' you! And what the hell happened to your face? Whatever it was, your cheatin' ass deserves it! What, her nigga got a hold of you last night when you was with her and not at home!" Taj screamed as she ran through the front room to the kitchen. Since Prime wouldn't give her keys back to her, she snatched his off the kitchen counter and rushed out the door.

"Taj! Taj!" he screamed, running behind her like a little lost puppy, till he fell over his own feet as he tried to run out the door. By the time he got up from the wet grass, Taj was already speeding out of the driveway in his truck. He cursed as the truck disappeared into the darkness of night, then he turned around and went back inside. For a second, he considered getting in her BMW and giving chase, but then he realized it was probably best to just let her calm down. She'll be back eventually. She needs clothes for work in the morning, he told himself.

Taj cried as she navigated the truck through the late night traffic. She drove around without a destination, just needing time to think. Her phone clipped to her side vibrated relentlessly. She looked at it and saw that it was Prime, then turned it off. Rivers of tears flowed down her face as she thought about all the plans they had made. *And now it's just…over. Damn him!*

* * * * *

As he was exiting the Quik Mart with his partner, Clue, Banta Man almost dropped the snacks and Swisher Sweets he was holding as he frantically dialed Rude Boy on his phone. "Yo, Rude Boy, guess who just pulled up in the gas station, mon," Banta Man said.

"Who, mon?" Rude Boy asked as he sat on his custom leather sofa, smoking weed from a bong.

"That nigga Prime's truck just turned into the lot. What you want me to do 'bout it, mon?" Banta Man asked as he watched the truck pull up to one of the gas pumps.

"Snatch his ass up and hold 'im for me, mon. I got somethin' special for that boy. Take 'im out to the house on Barge road," Rude Boy said going into a coughing fit.

"I got you, mon," Banta Man replied. He jumped into the Econoline van and pulled it over next to the pump behind Prime's truck.

"Hit me when the deed is done," Rude Boy said before he took another hit off the bong.

"I got you, mon," Banta Man assured him, then clicked the phone off. He put the van in park, eyed the lot around him, then said to Clue, "Hey, pass me my strap, man."

"What's up?" Clue said, handing him the gun.

"Just some business for the boss." Banta Man quickly clicked the safety off and tucked the locked and loaded weapon into his waistband. "We about to take care of that nigga Prime."

Just as he was plotting his next move, Taj stepped out of the truck.

Banta Man and Clue did a double-take to look at the well-built, chocolate mare. They watched Taj climb out, pump her gas, then go in the store to pay the clerk.

"It ain't that bitch-ass nigga after all! That bitch is bad, though, man!" Clue said, hungrily staring as Taj's ample ass flopped from side to side when she walked back to the truck.

Banta Man ran a couple scenarios through his head before he made his next move while keeping his eyes on Taj. "You drive," Banta Man told Clue, then opened his door and climbed out. He quickly eased over to Prime's truck before Taj got back and sneaked into the extended cab door. He squeezed in behind the driver seat and patiently waited for Taj to reach the truck. He knew Rude Boy would be just as happy to have the girl, because they could use her as bait to lure Prime in. He pulled his gun from his waistband and held it tight in his grip as he peeped around the seat, looking for Taj.

A few minutes later, Taj was climbing in the truck, still crying and hurt by Prime's supposed cheating, so distraught that she didn't even notice Banta Man in the back seat of the truck. She pulled the truck in drive and pulled out, paying no attention to the van that followed her turn by turn.

* * * * *

I sat around the room flipping through the channels until I got bored. I reached over, picked up the phone, and turned it on, hoping I'd missed call or text from Prime, but there were no messages or missed calls at all—not even from Katasha, Fat Fat, or Trent.

I laid my phone down, thought for a minute, then got up and slipped into the other outfit I'd bought at the mall. I pulled my hair back in a long ponytail, then ran the comb through my Chinese bangs. I puckered my lips and smoothed on some lipstick.

On my way out, I looked hopefully at my phone again, but there were still no calls or messages, so I tucked it in my pocket and exited the room. I climbed behind the wheel of the Challenger and guided it slowly out into the night traffic. I'd heard so much about Atlanta and its nightlife, and I couldn't wait to experience it firsthand. I didn't know my way around yet, but I remembered a club everyone had been talking about. I entered "Shakers" into my GPS while I waited at a red light, and then I navigated carefully to the hottest strip club in the city. When I pulled up in the lot, all I saw were a bunch of expensive, customized cars that I was sure had to cost six figures. I parked off to the side, checked my face in the mirror once more, then got out.

"Damn, shawty! Can't wait to see that ass naked," a heavy-set, ugly nigga called out, trying to show off for the other two unattractive men who were walking with him.

I ignored him as I walked in front of them up to the club entrance. I began digging in my pocket to pay the cover charge, but the girl behind the counter continued yapping on her phone and waved me on through. I overheard bits of her conversation as I walked by.

"Yeah, girl, these li'l heffas gettin' younger and younger up in here, shakin' they young asses for the almighty dollar. Ain't no way in the hell I could do that!" She laughed as she discreetly cut her eyes in my direction, obviously thinking I was one of the dancers.

I held my head high and walked on in as if I hadn't overheard her. The massive sound system pierced my ears, and the scene was like a big party, though many of the women were naked, except for their heels, none of which were shorter than three inches. I moved to the side to let one girl through; she was dressed down like me and was carrying a bag, so I assumed she was just getting to work. A few minutes later, a few more girls with bags entered and made their way back to the back, an indication that the nightshift was starting. Minutes later, those same girls were back on the floor in six-inch heels, half-dressed and ready to get naked for all the hustlers and ballers who were drinking and throwing money in the air.

"You must be the new girl," a tall, black and Asian woman said, moving a strand of hair out of her face. She immediately put me in the mind of Kimora Lee Simmons but with a lot more hips and ass. The woman had it going on, and I was sure every nigga in the club wanted a piece of her.

"Um, no," I replied, a bit flattered that she and the front desk girl had mistaken me for one of the sexy, attractive women who worked there.

"Oh. Sorry," she apologized, looking me up and down.

"No problem," I said, watching the dancers slither their naked bodies to Ciara's beats that were blasting from the sound system.

She looked at me sideways, with her nose in the air, probably wondering why I'd dressed in sneakers to attend the hottest strip club in the city. "You lookin' for work, honey?" she asked. "You don't look like you're from around here."

"I'm not from around here, but I'm not looking for work either. I'm just out chillin', having some me time," I said, still scanning the club.

"Oh, okay. You wanna dance?" she invited.

"Nah, I'm good," I said, irritated that she'd taken me for a lesbian or a bisexual.

She rolled her eyes at me. "Damn, girl. You ain't gotta be all like that. You do know this is a strip club, right?" she snapped.

"Yeah. I don't mean no disrespect. I'm just trying to chill out, that's all," I said, noticing the huge diamonds on her wrist and fingers.

"Where you from?" she asked, pulling at her bikini bottoms that were wedged in her oversized ass.

"Chicago."

Her eyes lit up. "What!? Girl, not the Chi! Me too, south side MLK, down off Drew Drive," she said excitedly.

I knew the area well, but it wasn't a side of the city anyone would want to be caught in. "Okay then, home girl!" I said, excited to meet someone from my hometown.

"You stayin' here now?" she asked. "And my name's Fiz," she said.

All of the sudden, a tall, brown-skinned brother sporting enough jewelry to open up a jewelry store walked up. "Excuse me, ladies. Sorry to interrupt, but I was wondering if I could get a dance," he said to Fiz, taking in her thick, perfect figure.

Fiz looked him over, focusing on his big bling, then smiled. "I'm sure that can be arranged," she said. "Uh…" she said, looking at me, clearly wanting to know my name.

"Nikki," I said.

"Nikki, why don't you hang around for a minute?" she said, turning her attention back to the baller.

"A'ight," I said.

She smiled and walked away behind the brother, throwing her big ass from side to side, making sure that everyone noticed her.

I found an empty table in the back, ordered a drink, and watched as men and woman threw their money at the heavily made-up girls who were trying to make a living with their bodies. I laughed to myself at all the wannabe players and hustlers trying to outshine one another.

"Hi. How you doin'?" a short, curly-haired, fat man in a two-piece suit said as he sat in the chair next to me.

Before I could answer, I heard a loud commotion. When I looked toward the front of the club, I saw that all the yelling and screaming was the crowd rooting on two young, attractive dancers as they simulated sex acts with each other. The crowd went wild when one of the girls started to actually eat the other girl out.

CHAPTER 10

Taj made a left on Maplewood Drive, the backstreet that bypassed downtown Decatur; in her back seat, still unbeknownst to her, Banta Man was still hiding quietly. As she drove through the dark neighborhood, Taj noticed a van behind her, making every turn she made. Just to make sure she wasn't being paranoid or that she wasn't mistaken, she made a quick right at the next corner, then a quick left at the light, without signaling. She looked in her rearview mirror and saw that the van was still behind her.

When Taj brought the truck to a slow roll on top of the next hill and stopped, Banta Man made his move. Just as she pressed the gas pedal to proceed, a hand snaked around her neck from behind.

"Ah!" she screamed slamming on the brakes, bringing the truck to a quick halt.

The pursuing van sped up and stopped next to the truck while she struggled to get out of the truck and away from the intruder.

"Bitch, stay still and don't fuckin' move!" Banta Man screamed, pulling his gun out and sticking it in her face.

Taj stopped struggling immediately.

Banta Man reached up and threw the truck into park.

"Please don't kill me! God, please help me!" Taj cried, shaking uncontrollably as the man in the van jumped out and rushed over to the truck.

"Shut the fuck up!" Banta Man screamed, holding Taj roughly by the hair and ramming the gun into her cheek.

Clue ran over, jerked the truck door open, and pulled Taj out, then slammed her to the concrete, face first.

"Ow! Oh please!" Taj cried out.

Clue stood over her and hit her with a closed fist, knocking her out cold.

"Hurry up and get the bitch in the van," Banta Man told Clue as he climbed over the seat and got behind the wheel of the truck.

Clue picked up the small Taj and carried her over to the van like a sack of potatoes. After securing her in the back, he pulled out and followed Banta Man out to Rude Boy's stash-house out on Barge Road. Thirty minutes later, they pulled up to the house on a dead-end street.

"Let's get her inside," Banta Man said, opening the van door.

They locked Taj in the back room of the cold, dark house, then called Rude Boy.

"Yo, mon, we didn't get Prime, but—" Banta Man started but was cut off by a screaming Rude Boy.

"What!? Why you callin' me if you ain't got him, mon? What in the hell happened?" Rude Boy yelled, pacing back and forth in his west side townhouse.

"Be cool, mon! Prime wasn't in the truck, but some bitch was, so we grabbed her. We good, mon. She's gotta be his bitch. She's in the back now, knocked the fuck out," Banta said, watching Clue pull a plastic bag of sticky green out of his pocket.

"You sure she's his lady?" Rude Boy asked in a sinister tone, smiling evilly from ear to ear.

"I think so, mon," Banta Man replied, passing Clue the Swisher Sweets he'd bought at the gas station.

"I'm on my way," Rude Boy said, ending the call.

* * * * *

"Where she at?" Rude Boy said as soon as he stormed into the house.

"In the back," Clue replied as he closed the door, "still blacked out."

Rude Boy hurried to the back room, walked over to the unconscious Taj, and grabbed the phone that was clipped to her side. He looked through it and saw a lot of recent missed calls from a number Rude Boy knew well, calls and texts from Prime that had gone unnoticed or ignored. When he read the texts, he realized that Taj was, in fact, Prime's woman, and the two of them were in the middle of a nasty domestic dispute. He tucked the phone and looked over at Taj, then began to rub his dick when he caught sight of her plump backside and thick thighs in her tight leggings. The weed and liquor he'd been drinking and smoking all day had him high and horny. "I'ma send our friend Prime a message he'll never forget," Rude Boy slurred as he started unbuckling his pants.

"Ha! Yeah, mon, that nigga gon' learn now!" Banta Man

laughed a loud, toothy chuckle as Clue fired up another blunt.

They all stood in the back room smoking weed and lusting over Taj, who was still laid out on her stomach, completely unaware of where she was or what danger she was in.

"Gimme ya blade, mon," Rude Boy said.

Banta Man quickly produced his razor-sharp knife from his back pocket

While Banta Man and Clue passed the blunt, Rude Boy leaned over Taj with the knife tight in his grip. "Video this for me, mon," he said, pulling Taj's phone from his pocket and passing it to Clue. He then waited until Clue had the camera phone in position before he carried on.

"Action!" Clue called out, laughing and prompting Rude Boy to start the show.

Rude Boy used the blade to carefully slit Taj's tights down the back.

"No panties, mon!" Banta Man called out while exhaling the blunt smoke.

Rude Boy's dick grew rock hard at the sight of Taj's smooth, blemish-free, plump ass. He ran his large, ashy hand between her butt cheeks, down to her hairless center. Taj squirmed a little when Rude Boy jammed his big, long fingers into her. He pulled his hand out, spat on his finger, then stuck it back in; this time it slid in freely.

Taj's eyes popped open as Rude Boy climbed onto her. She turned around and started screaming at the top of her lungs as Rude Boy pinned her to the mattress with his body weight. "Ah! Nooooo!" As her head cleared a bit, she suddenly remembered the man in the back of the truck and the van that had been following her. "Who are you? Get off of me!"

"Aw, bitch, I'm about to get off all right!" Rude Boy yelled as he used one hand to press her head into the mattress and the other to guide his rock-hard dick into her.

"Please no!" Taj cried, trying to fight him off, to no avail.

Rude Boy handled Taj with ease as Clue made sure he got it all on video. "This is for your man Prime!" he called out, looking into the camera while ramming his cock into a crying Taj, hard and rough.

"Ow! Stop! Please!" Taj screamed out in pain.

After he'd made a few hard thrusts, Taj's insides grew moist, making Rude Boy's intrusion that much easier. He slid in and out real easy, moaning out in ecstasy as he continued to violate Taj in the worst way. A few pumps later, he was spilling his hot juices inside of her.

Taj lay there stiff as a board, crying and hoping her nightmare would end soon.

"Damn. That's some good pussy!" Rude Boy slapped her ass as he pulled out.

"I got it all on here. You next, Banta Man?" Clue asked, resetting the video on the phone.

"Hold on. Let's get Prime on the line first," Rude Boy ordered as he fixed his clothes.

Taj lay curled up in a ball, crying and sobbing as the three men used her phone to call Prime.

The ringing of Prime's phone woke him up immediately, and he hurried to grab it before it went to voicemail. He was glad to see that it was Taj calling. "Taj, baby, where you at?" he asked sleepily, hoping she'd calmed down and was on her way back home.

"I ain't your baby, mon. I want me money, and now you'll pay double what you owe, plus interest…if you still want your lady friend back when we're through with her. I want

$150,000 in the next twenty-four hours, or she's dead. By the way, she's got some good pussy, mon," Rude Boy said, then busted out laughing.

Prime's heart dropped into his stomach. He couldn't believe Rude Boy had his baby, his heart, the love of his life. "You touch her, and I'm gonna fuckin' kill you and every-fuckin'-body you know! I got your damn money! Put Taj on the phone, man," Prime said, wide awake and climbing off the bed. He was furious and couldn't help but to blame himself for what was happening.

"Hold up, mon. You don't get to make no fuckin' demands! Listen, you pussy muthafucker, you better get me money in twenty-four hours, or this bitch is dead! While you getting me money, I got a li'l somethin' for you to watch." Rude Boy laughed, then clicked off the line. He fumbled with the phone for a moment trying to figure out how to send the video. A few minutes after he pressed the send button, a call came through. Rude Boy looked at it, smiled, and pressed the button to answer it.

"Man, please! Please don't hurt her no mo', Rude Boy. I swear I'm gonna get your money. We ain't gotta do it like this, my nigga. Come on, man. It's a simple misunderstanding, that's all. Let me holla at her, man." Prime's eyes began to water as he thought about Rude Boy violating his baby girl; until that night, Taj had never been with anyone but him.

"Are you bawlin' like a bitch, mon?" Rude Boy teased. "Not so tough now, are ya?" Rude Boy then threw the cell phone on the bed next to Taj, who quickly grabbed it.

"Please give 'em whatever they want, Prime. Please get me out of here! I can't take—" Taj whined, but she was quickly cut short.

NIKKI

Smack!

Rude Boy slapped Taj hard across the face, sending the phone flying across the room.

Prime cringed on the other end, with only murder on his mind.

"Uh!" Taj cried out as Rude Boy laughed and picked up the phone from the floor.

Prime heard the other men in the background, and that only made him angrier.

"Get me money!" Rude Boy growled, then ended the call.

Prime's chest grew tight, and his blood pressure rose as he thought about what Rude Boy was doing to her. He blamed himself over and over again for what was happening to Taj as he slipped his shoes on. Prime had never been the soft type, but seeing Rude Boy raping his baby girl on the video brought tears to his eyes. He went to the closet, pulled out all the money he had, and realized he was way short of the $150,000 Rude Boy was demanding. He paced the room, ready to kill, then grabbed his phone off the nightstand and quickly dialed.

* * * * *

"Hello?" I answered, trying to hear him over the loud club music.

"Say, Nikki, I need your help," Prime said shakily, trying to keep his cool.

"Prime? You okay?" I asked, feeling the effects of the two drinks I'd polished off a bit too quickly.

"I need you to meet me at the room right now," Prime said in a firm tone.

"Um, okay. I'm on my way," I replied, then hung up. I got

up and looked around the packed club, trying to spot Fiz, who still hadn't returned to the table. I circled the club until I found Fiz, who was busy giving a young hustler a lap dance. "Hit me up. I gotta go." I said, handing her a napkin with my number written on it.

"I got you, home girl." Fiz winked as she bounced up and down hard in the boy's lap, giving him his money's worth.

* * * * *

When I pulled up at the hotel, Prime was already there, sitting out front in a BMW. "What's wrong, Prime?" I asked.

He stepped out the car, looking worried. "I need that money we made off the work today. Them niggas done snatched up my lady and are gonna kill her if I don't pay them $150,000," he said, looking at me as if it was an offer I couldn't refuse.

I paused, looked around the dark parking lot, then took a deep breath. "Um…okay."

CHAPTER 11

"I told you it's good, mon!" Rude Boy called out as Banta Man released inside of Taj.

She was now numb to the men who were taking turns raping her; Rude Boy had even gone back for sloppy seconds. Taj's tears had turned to anger as she was repeatedly humped like a dog. The anger in her heart was directed more at Prime than her captors and rapists, though, because she knew it was all his fault; in that moment, she hated Prime as much as she hated the men who were violating her. She silently prayed that the men would get tired and stop. Their stench of sex and sweat and weed made her gag and throw up, but even that didn't stop them; they paid her vomit no mind and just continued doing whatever they wanted to do to her.

"Fuck yeah, mon!" Banta Man called out as he wiped his dick off on Taj's shirt.

"Pass the blunt, mon!" Rude Boy told Clue. When his phone began to ring, he looked down at it and started smiling, revealing his gold teeth. "Yeah, mon!" he said, noticing Prime's number on the caller ID. "Boy's got me money now!"

"Look, Rude Boy, I got a li'l over half of what you want, and I'm gonna give your dope back. Where you wanna do this?" Prime said, standing next to me at the table, staring at all the money I had, as well as the piles of dope that were left.

When Prime had come demanding my share of the money, at first I had been pissed, but apart from being scared to refuse, I also saw the worry and hurt in his face. Besides, he had promised to pay me back by the end of the week.

"Meet me at the Discount Mall out on Old National Highway. We can make the exchange there," Rude Boy said to Prime.

"Okay. I'll be there in twenty minutes," Prime said, looking over at me.

"A'ight, but any police or funny business, and the girl's dead. We on our way." With that, Rude Boy closed the phone, ending the call.

* * * * *

Rude Boy and Banta Man smoked a blunt and gave Clue an extra five minutes for another round with the bleeding, dazed Taj as they went over their plans.

"Get the girl, and let's go," Rude Boy said to Clue when he finally exited the room, buckling his pants. He then grabbed his .45 automatic and Prime's keys off the table.

Banta Man and Clue grabbed Taj and carried her out to the van.

She was unable to stand or walk from the rough pounding she'd taken, and she wiped tears away as they pushed her to the floor of the van and slammed the door behind her.

Rude Boy climbed behind the wheel of Prime's truck and followed them out to the south side of Atlanta to collect.

When they arrived at the meeting place, they found Prime sitting behind the wheel of the BMW parked in the far end of the lot. Rude Boy and Banta Man pulled to the opposite side and parked.

Prime opened the door of his fiancée's car and stepped out with a bag in his hand and a hard scowl on his face.

Rude Boy got out of Prime's truck and slowly made his way across the dark, deserted lot with his .45 in reach.

Banta Man and Clue pulled Taj out of the van and held her.

"I got your money and dope right here. Let her go, man," Prime said with attitude, looking across the lot at Banta Man and Clue, who were holding a frightened, destroyed, weeping Taj in between them.

Rude Boy smiled, revealing his grill; it humored him to see Prime suffer.

"Do I need to inspect it?" Rude Boy asked, standing face to face with Prime.

Prime held his anger as he kept his eyes on Taj across the lot. "It don't matter. It's all there," Prime replied, loosening his grip on the bag.

Rude Boy grabbed the bag, looked in it, then raised his hand in the air.

"I'm gonna trust you this time," Rude Boy said as Banta Man and Clue followed the instructions when the signal was made.

"Yeah, okay," Prime said, about to walk around Rude Boy.

"Hold up. Let's call it even," Rude Boy said sarcastically, sticking his hand out for a shake.

Prime looked at Rude Boy with daggers in his eyes, then

looked down at the gun he had tucked in his waistband. Knowing he was outnumbered and outgunned, he reluctantly stuck his hand out and shook Rude Boy's, even though he would have preferred to put a bullet in his head.

Rude Boy turned and walked back across the lot with Prime following a few feet behind him.

Clue and Banta Man had put Taj in Prime's truck and then gotten back in the van to wait for Rude Boy. Rude Boy climbed in the van, and seconds later, Clue was whipping the Econoline out of the lot.

Prime walked briskly to his truck as he watched the van disappear into the darkness. He jerked the truck door open, glad to have his baby girl back. When he got in and looked at her, though, it was as if his whole world ended right that moment. Taj was lying in the seat, dead, with her throat slashed from ear to ear. "Baby? Taj? No!" Prime screamed.

In a daze, he opened the truck door and crawled out, holding his chest. "You mines, nigga! You mines!" Prime screamed, waving his fist in the air.

He then carefully gathered Taj up, gently placed her in her car, dialed 911, and hurried back to his truck before the police showed up.

CHAPTER 12

Knock! Knock! Knock!

I rolled over, half-asleep. "Yeah?" I said, climbing out of bed and wondering who was at my door in the middle of the night. I looked out the peephole and saw Prime's truck out front. I thought sure he'd get his lady back and stay in for the night, so I wondered what he was doing there. When I opened the door and looked up in his eyes, I instantly knew something was wrong. "You didn't get her?" I asked.

He marched past me with his head down, then sat down on the bed and dropped his head in his hands. "No. They…those muthafuckers killed her," Prime mumbled as he wiped tears from his eyes.

My heart dropped. "Oh no. Prime, I-I'm sorry." I walked over and sat next to him on the bed. My heart went out to him. In the short time we'd known each other, I had never seen his sensitive side, but seeing him shed tears for his lost love had me tearing up myself. It was obvious that he loved and cared for her deeply. When I looked at him, I couldn't help thinking back on my own painful loss of my parents.

"I swear I'm gonna get them niggas." He sniffed, then inhaled deeply.

"I can't believe they killed her. Damn," I said, somewhat nervous about being around him when he was so enraged. Really, I was at a loss for words, unsure of what to do or say. I rubbed my hand across his back to comfort him while he let it all out.

A few minutes later, he was lying back on the bed, asleep. I pulled his shoes off, put his legs up on the bed, and climbed in next to him. I watched him sleep until I joined him in a deep slumber.

* * * * *

The sun shone through the hotel room as Prime climbed out of bed.

I wiped my eyes and sat up. "You okay?" I asked as he walked back to the bathroom to relieve himself.

"Yeah," he answered quietly before he entered the bathroom.

I wanted to ask him about the money, but under the circumstances, I wasn't sure how to bring it up. He hadn't filled me in on the details of the exchange, other than his girlfriend's murder, I felt really bad for him, but at the same time, I needed money to live on. When I'd finally gotten the nerve up to ask him, I threw the covers back and climbed out of bed. "So, uh... what's next, Prime? I mean, did you...did they get the money and the dope or what?" I asked hesitantly as I went to the sink to wash my face.

He paused, stared at me, then walked to the window. "I'm

get yo' money," he said with a hint of attitude in his tone while peeking out between the curtains.

I turned my head away from him and rolled my eyes. "Well, you know I don't have money for this room, and I can't keep driving around in a stolen car. I know this is bad timing and all, but I just don't know what I'm gonna do now," I said, feeling slightly stupid for trusting him and letting his drama affect my ability to take care of myself.

"Grab your stuff from the car," he said before he walked over to the sink and splashed some water on his own face.

I didn't question him and just picked up my few possessions from the room and exited.

He came out behind me, carrying the rest of the dope. He helped me pack all my stuff in the truck, and thirty minutes later we were on our way to Rex, Georgia, a rural spot on the outskirts of Atlanta, to a two-bedroom home Prime's grandmother had left for him in her Will, a place he used to stash product from time to time.

Little did I know when we pulled up to that house that my life would never, ever be the same—and neither would Prime's.

CHAPTER 13

Living the fast life, one year later...

"Is this the only style you got in this shade of red?" Fiz asked the Gucci store salesman as she checked out the new bag selection.

"Absolutely not. Just follow me!" The man eagerly helped, looking for a hefty commission on the sale.

I looked down at my diamond-filled Rolex and saw that it was nearing 3:00. "Girl, c'mon. You know we gotta get down to Diva Palace to get our hair done. How many more bags do you need anyway? Shit, you already got every style and color Gucci makes," I said playfully as the salesman showed her the other bags.

Fiz turned and looked at me, placing her hand on her hip. "Look here, Miss Thang. You're gonna learn that you can never have enough bags, especially when you ain't the one buying them." She rolled her eyes playfully as she whipped out Jarvis's credit card, happy that he'd added her as an authorized user on.

Fiz was my girl. After Prime and I moved out to his grandmother's house in Rex, us two girls really started hanging strong. We had some of the same taste and were both from the Chi, and all the things we had in common only made us closer. Our five-year age difference wasn't a factor because I was well beyond my years both mentally and physically.

Prime and I had gotten real close since the move, but we hadn't crossed the line I was more than ready to cross. He'd seemed kind of distant and closed off since Taj's death, but his hustle never stopped. After we moved shop to Rex, Prime's game really took off. He flipped the last of the dope we had into close to a million, then moved us out to Gwinnett, into a $400,000 home. It was really confusing at times; I wasn't sure if I was just his business partner, somebody to keep him company, or his lady. I was bombarded with mixed signals daily, but I just went with the flow. We had an odd relationship, like a couple without any intimacy between us. If I didn't know about the Taj situation, I might have thought he was gay. I just sat back and stayed patient, though; he was still trying to deal with a heart-wrenching loss, and that was something I understood more than most.

"Teach, Fiz!" I said, laughing when she chose a fly $2,800 Gucci bag. I'd already spent $8,000 at the Lenox Mall, so I spared our bank account another big purchase; besides that, Prime wasn't bringing it in like Fiz's man Jarvis.

"I'm with that. Let's go get our sexy on." She snapped her finger in a circle as we exited to head to the salon.

We crossed the lot to Fiz's candy apple-red Benz wagon sitting on twenty-four-inch custom rims, a gift from Jarvis. Fiz was a gorgeous woman, and she had it going on with her long, thick, expensive weaves, perfect body, and slanted eyes she'd inherited from her father. Men were crazy about Fiz, and she knew it; that was why she kept her nose in the air unless they were making big money. She was a gold-digger, plain and simple, and she didn't care who knew it.

"We gonna have to make a trip home one weekend. I'd love to see what the city looks like after all these years," she said, easing the Benz wagon out into the mounting traffic.

"Yeah, we're gonna have to do that," I said, even though I wasn't about to step foot back in Chicago until I found out what was up with Trent.

"How 'bout we fly out this weekend?" she suggested, ready to make the trip.

"Girl, I can't go back to the Chi right now," I said, wondering what Katasha and Fat Fat were up to.

"Why not? Prime got you all like that?" She looked at me over her Prada aviators.

"Girl, ain't no man got me like that," I shot back, rolling my neck.

"Well, then let's go," she persisted.

Fiz was my girl, and I felt like I could really trust her. I knew she would stay on my back about it until I gave her my reasons for not wanting to go back to The Windy City just yet.

"Do you know a nigga name Trent from the south side? I think he's from Dell Avenue, or at least he gets money out that way. He's a cute-ass nigga with good hair," I said, remembering what Fat Fat had told me about Trent.

"Hell naw! You know Trent, the one with the dimples, thick eyebrows, sexy as hell? That nigga grew up right across the street from me. Used to run with my cousin Moe. I think they still tight till this day. Last time I talked to Moe, 'bout two years ago, they was still doing their thang. Damn, that brings back some memories, girl. I had the biggest crush on Trent when we were young," she replied excitedly.

After gauging her reaction, I considered keeping my secrets to myself, but after I thought about it for a minute, I decided to go ahead and fill her in.

"Fiz, I did some shit that would probably get me killed if I went back to Chicago right now," I said softly.

"Huh? Get you killed? Damn, girl, what happened?" she asked with a concerned look on her face.

I didn't spare a detail as I told her my life story, from getting put out to stealing Trent's car.

"Hmm. It's all good. Fuck it. Let's just take a trip to Miami. I'm ready to see my boo anyway. Fuck Chicago. It's too cold up that bitch to be visiting anyway," she said, smiling.

I smiled right back at her. Fiz was my girl, and going to Miami sounded real good.

CHAPTER 14

"**H**ow in the hell am I gonna make anything off this shit at that price? Why the hell does shit cost almost double? There ain't no shortage in the street, is there?" Prime asked Chavez, his drug connect.

Prime had always thought Chavez was the man, but now he knew otherwise. Chavez turned out to be only a middle man, and now that he was in debt with the boss, he was raising the prices to make up the money he owed. "There's a drought, man—and on top of that, my transport fee has increased. You know how business goes. When my price on handling this shit goes up, the price of the product does too. Don't fret though. It won't be this way for long, 'cause I'm working on some things to make life better for both of us. In due time, I'll be givin' you this shit dirt cheap, but right now, $42,000 a kilo is the best I can do, no matter how many you cop."

Prime wiped the sweat from his forehead, just finishing up his daily workout. He couldn't believe that even buying ten kilos a drop, he still had to pay top dollar. "Damn, Chavez! That's kinda rich for my blood. Just gimme a minute, and I'll get back at you."

As soon as Prime hung up, he dialed another number. He made four more calls altogether but still couldn't reach anyone to see if he could get a better price. He undressed and headed to the shower.

Beep! Beep! Beep!

"Yeah?" he answered, agitated.

"Hey, handsome. What's wrong?" I asked, instantly noticing the anger and frustration in his tone.

"Hey, baby. My bad. This wetback's tryin'a charge me damn near triple, and I ain't feeling it. My people'll be hittin' anytime now, ready to spend, and I ain't got shit for 'em," he said, pissed.

"That's messed up. Lemme holla at Fiz. Her dude's on that level. I'll talk to you about it when I get home," I said as Carmen, my stylist, led me to the salon chair.

"Okay," he replied.

"Love you."

"Love you too," he said dryly.

He said those three little words every now and then, never with much emotion, but I didn't trip; I knew the Taj situation was still weighing heavily on him, and he still felt guilty about her rape and murder. I was determined to help him get over her, but the more I pushed, the more he sank deeper into his regrets. I knew I had to be patient and just hoped he'd officially make me his by making love to me one day, something that was long overdue. I had tried everything to get him worked up as we lay in each other's arms every night, but it always ended with a kiss on the neck and a soft-spoken "Goodnight."

Prime got dressed, grabbed his Glock, and exited the house. He hopped in his new Benz SL600. He tossed the bag of money on the back seat and headed out to the Bluff, one of the grimiest parts of Atlanta, where the Reaper resided. The bag contained

$40,000, the amount the Reaper wanted to take care of Rude Boy and Banta Man, $20,000 a head.

CHAPTER 15

"Excuse me, brother. Can you spare some change?" the shabbily dressed black woman asked as she walked up on the truck where Rude Boy and Banta Man sat counting the money they'd just collected from their hotel crew.

Banta Man stopped counting and looked at her, curling his lip up in disgust. "Get the fuck away from the truck. We ain't got no money fo' yo' ass!" he yelled from behind the wheel of Rude Boy's truck.

The woman almost dropped the plastic jug she was holding out when he screamed at her. "Man, c'mon! I just need a li'l change to get somethin' to eat. Help a sista out, man," she begged, stepping right up to the window.

Banta Man stopped counting the money and looked up at her in disbelief. He frowned and stuck his head out the window, getting right in her face. "Can't you hear, woman? No change! Now get the fuck—"

His words were cut off as he screamed out in pain, the boric acid from her jug burning the flesh right off his face, melting him like a flame to a candle.

"Ah!" he screamed, running his hands over his dissolving face, only to wiped away clumps of burnt, disintegrating flesh.

"What the fuck, mon!" Rude Boy screamed as Banta Man pulled back into the truck window, his face nothing more than a bloody pulp.

Without another word, the woman pulled an ice pick out of her jacket with lightning speed, leaned over into the truck, and buried it in Banta Man's chest, puncturing his heart.

Rude Boy fumbled with the door handle until he got the door open, but just as he struck out running, the Reaper rounded the truck and stayed right on his heels as he hurried through a heavily wooded lot that led to a train cargo yard. Rude Boy ran as fast as he could, but he couldn't shake the Reaper; she moved with stealth, dodging hanging branches and fallen trees as if they weren't even there.

"Who are you? What's your beef?" Rude Boy screamed as he crossed the first set of railroad tracks that ran through the freight yard.

Boom!

The blast from the .357 pierced the Reaper's eardrum. The loud yelp up ahead let her know she'd hit her intended target. The Reaper slowed her run to a steady trot until she was standing over Rude Boy, who was lying between the railroad tracks writhing in pain, taken down when the bullet ripped through his leg.

"Please wait! What you want, girl? Cash? I got plenty a money for you!" Rude Boy yelled, holding his bloody leg as tight as he could.

Boom!

That second shot tore through his other leg.

"Ow! Oh mi God! You crazy bitch! Wait! Wait! What is it?" he yelled, trying to claw away.

In the distance, a train whistle sounded, and a sparkle of delight glistened in the Reaper's eye. Rude Boy was too busy screaming and trying to get away to hear the oncoming train. The Reaper pulled the cell phone Prime had given her to record a video. Rude Boy paused and looked up at the Reaper, wondering why she was aiming the phone at him. "I hear you like to put on for the camera," she said, then laughed hysterically.

All of a sudden, it hit him. *Prime's bitch*, he thought. "Please no!" Rude Boy called out as the train neared. At that point, he finally heard the train coming his way. The closer it got, the more the tracks vibrated under his bloody, shredded legs. He somehow managed to crawl off the tracks as the vibration got harder.

The Reaper videoed him as he cried out in pain, pleading that his life would be spared. Just as the train came into view, the Reaper walked over to Rude Boy, put the phone in her pocket, and pulled out her .357.

Boom! Boom!

The two carefully placed shots ripped through his body, one breaking his hip and the other puncturing his stomach.

Rude Boy screamed out in excruciating pain. "Ah! Come on, mon! Please have mercy!" he yelled.

The Reaper calmly walked over, grabbed him by his ankles, and maneuvered him back onto the tracks, smiling all the while.

"No! Please!" Rude Boy called out again. He fought with all his might to get off the tracks, but the blood loss and pain rendered him helpless.

The Reaper stood back, pulled the phone out again, and recorded as the freight train barreled down the track at full speed. The train conductor couldn't pull the brakes fast enough, and at least 120 tons of metal collided with Rude Boy's body, tearing him to pieces. His mangled body was dragged down the track for a couple miles before the train came to a screeching, sparking halt.

With the video proof Prime had asked for, she made her way back through the woods and to the hotel parking lot. She walked over to the truck and snapped a photo of the bloody, faceless, dead Banta Man sprawled out on the seat, and then, like the phantom she was named after, she disappeared around the corner in the darkness.

Prime was sleeping like a baby when his ringing phone woke him up. He grabbed it from the nightstand and noticed that he had two missed calls, a text, picture, and a video message. The text read, "Done." When he opened the photo, he had to look away because Banta Man's remains were so gruesome, almost unrecognizable. He then played the video, which made him cringe. After looking at the picture and the video again, he smiled. He had sworn he wouldn't rest until he'd avenged Taj's death. Now that both men were dead, his beloved could rest in peace.

I stirred as I felt him kiss my back and neck. A few seconds later, he was on top of me, slowly sliding his fat hard-on inside of my moist center. I didn't know what had come over him, but I wasn't about to stop him; it felt so good that it brought tears to my eyes, like I'd died and gone to Heaven.

CHAPTER 16

Sunday rolled around, and I had the grill smoking like a chimney. Prime and I had invited some friends over for a barbecue and to watch the game, though the real purpose was for Prime to meet Jarvis, Fiz's man, so they could talk business. I was eager to meet Jarvis myself. I had spoken to the man on several occasions, and Fiz talked about him twenty-four/seven, so I felt like I knew everything about him—his favorite food, his pet peeves, and even his favorite sexual position—but I had yet to meet him face to face. Fiz rambled on about him on the regular; I wasn't sure if the man himself impressed her or if it was his millions. Either way, since he'd just flown in from Miami and was going to be in town for the weekend, Fiz made sure he made time to meet us.

I didn't have a long guest list. I'd invited my stylist, who brought her man Casper along; he owned 770 Customs, a high-end car customization shop that catered to the stars. Prime had invited his childhood friend, Justin, who brought his white girlfriend.

As I sat there looking around at everyone, tipsy, hungry, and having a good time, I didn't regret my decision to move to the South one bit. Prime had really changed my life, and I was loving every minute of it.

Fiz called me to let me know she would be late because she'd just picked Jarvis up and was stuck in traffic. The rest of us chatted it up while we watched the pregame show, and a half-hour later, the doorbell rang.

"The man himself," I said as I opened the door for Fiz and Jarvis to enter.

"And you must be Nikki." He smiled a big, perfect grin, showing off his cosmetic dental job.

"The one and only," I replied, discreetly checking out the man who had my girl head over heels. Honestly, I found him quite attractive, and I couldn't really find one flaw. He was the spitting image of Rick Fox, not a day younger or older.

"Yep, this is my bestie," Fiz said, linking her arm in mine as they stepped in.

I noticed Jarvis giving me a slick inspection as well as we all headed to the room where everyone was waiting for the game to start. "Hey, everybody," I announced, "this is my girl Fiz, as some of you already know, and this is her man, Jarvis, who just flew in from Miami."

Everyone greeted each other, and Prime didn't waste any time in walking over to personally introduce himself to the man who controlled a quarter of the Miami drug trade. "Hey, how's it goin'? I'm Prime," he said, then offered his hand for a shake, knowing that Fiz had already spoken to him about the business proposition.

"All's well. Beautiful home you have here," Jarvis replied, shaking Prime's hand with a firm grip, showing his power in a subliminal way.

"Thanks, but with the prices I'm getting these days, I'll be under a bridge soon," Prime whispered. He tried to make it sound like a joke, but he was dead serious.

"Yeah, I've heard all about your situation. How about we enjoy some food and the game and talk numbers after that?" Jarvis suggested; not even business could interrupt a Miami Heat game, as far as he was concerned.

Prime nodded his head in agreement. "Sounds good," he said, eager to appease the man who could catapult him to the next level of the game.

A few minutes later, the basketball game was tipping off.

A few minutes into the first quarter, Prime's phone rang. "Yo, what's up?" he answered when he saw Big's number on the caller ID.

"What up, homey? I need to see ya," Big said from his position in front of JJ's Rib Shack, devouring a sandwich between words.

"Big, you know I don't do no moving on Sundays, man. It's the playoffs, fool," Prime said, moving himself away from the crowd, "and I got company to watch the game."

"Ooh!" everyone in the room called out as Dwyane Wade dunked.

"Bruh, look, I know it's the Sabbath and basketball and some shit, but I got my folks from Alabama here, and they need to shop before they head back today. I know how you move, my nigga. They was s'posed to be here yesterday, but they got caught up. Man, they willing to pay $46,000 a play since it's a desert down they way," Big explained, licking sauce from his thick fingers.

The $46,000/kilo offer made Prime pause and think twice. He had three kilos left, and the price he was forced to sell them for, since his own cost was so high, had made them hard to move. He did a quick calculation in his head and decided to go ahead and knock off what he could at the higher price. "A'ight, man. How many we talking?" he asked, hesitant to break his own rules.

"They want five," Big said, then took a swig of sweet tea.

"Shit. I'm only holdin' three."

"Damn. A'ight though. Just swing that."

"Make sure your people are in place at the usual spot. I need to be in and out," Prime said, hoping to make the transaction quick as possible.

"It's all good. I'll have everything ready and will handle it myself," Big replied.

Prime ended the call then stepped from the back of the room and excused himself as he made his way upstairs to grab the package.

I got up and followed him as he left the room. "What up, baby? Where you goin'?" I asked as he unlocked the closet in the hall where he kept his stash.

"I gotta go make a play right quick," he said, grabbing three kilos. His man, Eric, had already paid for the other two, so he tucked those back under the clothes and shoes. He then grabbed a backpack out of the closet and stuffed the three kilos in it.

I took a deep breath, stepped back, and rolled my eyes at him. "But it's Sunday, Prime. You don't work Sundays," I said, making sure he picked up on my attitude.

"I know, but you know the problem I been having moving this high-ass shit. I just got a play for the last three. It won't take but a minute," he said, taking me in his arms and kissing me softly on the lips.

"Just hurry, all right? And what's up with Jarvis?" I asked

curiously.

"Don't know yet. We're gonna talk business tonight after the game." He grabbed the bag and threw it over his shoulder.

"Oh, okay," I said as he turned and walked to the stairs. "Just make it quick...and be careful."

"Always, baby," he said, and then he was gone.

* * * * *

Prime pushed his Benz down 285 till he reached Campbelton Road. He picked up his cell phone and called Big to let him know he was just up the street from their usual meeting spot.

"That's what's up! I'm already out here," Big said, scanning the office strip parking lot.

Prime pulled up a few minutes later.

When Big spotted him, he got out of his car, walked over to Prime's vehicle, and got in.

"Nigga, you got me working on my day off," Prime joked.

Big looked around the parking lot suspiciously before he spoke up. "Boy, you know I appreciate you, fam'. Everything good?" he asked, always looking over his shoulder.

Prime frowned, looking at Big like he was crazy. "Nigga, what you mean? Man, come on wit' it, 'cause I gotta get back to the house. Like I told you before I came out, I gotta be in and out, and now you're askin' all these damn ques—" Prime spat, but Big cut him off.

"A'ight, a'ight!" Big opened the car door and stepped out.

"Hurry up, man! I told you to be on point!" Prime yelled as Big closed the door.

Prime had been serving Big for years. They'd both watched each other climb the ranks in the game, but Prime had far outdone his old finger-lickin' friend. He looked in his rearview mirror and watched as Big got back in his car and picked up his cell phone. Prime tapped his steering wheel impatiently, waiting for Big to return.

"Signal confirmed! Move in!" the Federal agent in charged barked into his radio.

In an instant, the men who were crouched low and out of sight behind cars in the lot were up and pointing guns at Prime, all of them dressed in black from head to toe, shouting and screaming and telling him not to move.

"Put your hands out the window now!" a hulking, over-weight agent yelled as the other agents surrounded the car with their guns drawn.

Prime instantly began to sweat. He looked into his rearview again, shaking his head. Big was gone. "Fuck!" he cursed as he stuck his hands out the window. He was furious that he'd broken his own rules and tried to make a transaction on Sunday. More so, though, he didn't want to believe his old friend from the 'hood had set him up, but now he knew better.

Seconds later, Prime was dragged out of the car and shoved, face first, onto the concrete. The agents roughly cuffed him, then placed him in the back of an unmarked police car. It didn't take them long to find the bag of three kilos in the backpack on the back seat of the Benz.

"Bingo! Let the lieutenant know our guy stood good on his word. We've got the big fish in custody, caught red-handed," the burly agent said as he climbed behind the wheel of the unmarked sedan, ready to take Prime down and book him.

* * * * *

It had gotten late, the game was over, and Prime still hadn't made it back home.

Fiz could tell by the look on my face that I was beyond worried. "Did you call him again? He'll be back in a minute, and in the meantime, we'll chill out for a while wit' you," she said, trying to comfort me.

I paced from the front room to the kitchen. I knew an hour was way more than enough time for Prime to have made the run. Two hours had passed, and he still hadn't made it back or returned any of my calls. I had a strong feeling that something was very, very wrong.

Crash!

Suddenly, there was a loud noise in the front of the house. Everyone rushed upstairs, only to come face to face with men dressed in all black, storming the house and carrying high-powered weapons.

"Federal agents! Everybody down!" the man with the big white "FBI" stenciled on the back of his shirt screamed as they leveled their guns on all of us.

"Federal agents?" I said shakily as the men ordered everybody to get down on the floor.

"Who is the owner of this house?" the agent asked, obviously looking for Prime's significant other.

"I-I am," I said, lifting my head to look up at the men.

The agent walked over and stood over me. "Here's our warrant," he said, shoving a signed search warrant in my face. "Now, I'm gonna need y'all to cooperate," he said with a heavy Southern drawl.

Minutes later, the men in black were all in action. During

their hour-long search of every nook and cranny of the house, they found the remaining two kilos in the upstairs closet, along with $80,000 cash. They lined all of us up and patted us down. Since my name was on the deed, I was arrested for possession. My guests just stood and watched as I was placed in the back of the police car and hauled off.

In the back of the cruiser, with handcuffs on my wrists, tears ran down my face. Unable to do anything else, I dropped my head and just prayed as we darted in and out of traffic.

CHAPTER 17

The next day, Prime was pulled from the holding cell where he'd spent the night tossing and turning on the bench. They escorted him to an interrogation room.

A few minutes later, a heavyset, black, balding Federal agent stepped into the cold, dreary, gray room. "Mr. Chris Collins, aka Prime. You like games, don't you? How 'bout we play one. Let's make a deal." He snatched the small folding metal chair from under the table and took a seat across the table from Prime, slapping a folder down in front of him and setting a Styrofoam cup of coffee beside it.

"Games? I don't know what the hell you're talkin' about," Prime said, sitting proudly in his chair and staring at the agent with a sly grin on his face.

Smack!

The agent slapped the table, causing the cup of coffee to shake and almost topple over. "Look, smartass. You give me the name of the piece of shit you get your shit from, and I'll get the prosecutor to cut your black ass some slack. Either that, or I can let her rip you to pieces for the shit we found in your car." With that threat, the agent gave him a similarly sly smile before he picked up his cup of coffee and took a sip.

Prime shifted in his chair, let out a light sigh, and smiled back. "I ain't got shit to do with what y'all found in that car," he said, sitting back in his chair and folding his arms across his chest.

The agent took another sip of his coffee, let out a light giggle, then leaned forward in his chair, getting right in Prime's face. "Look here, brother," he said emphatically, "right now, I own your ass, and if you want to save it from the reaming it'll no doubt get in lockup, you'd better be a good li'l boy and help me help you. If you're tryin' to call my bluff, if you think I'm bullshitting, just keep fooling around and watch what happens when you're found guilty. At a minimum, you're looking at thirty years to life," the agent said, then smiled victoriously.

"What you found in that car wasn't mine. Your snitch got in my car with that bag and left it, so I'm through talking," Prime hissed, then stared the agent down, knowing deep down that he was stuck between a rock and a hard spot.

The agent shook his head and stood up. "Fine, tough guy. Have it your way. I was just trying to help you. I'm gonna walk out that door and give you fifteen minutes to think things through. When I come back, you'll have your last chance to save your black ass." With that, the agent snatched up the folder and his coffee, pulled the door open, and walked out.

Prime kept his tough-guy persona on display up until the agent exited the room. As soon as the agent closed the door behind him, he dropped his head in his hands. He knew they had him dead to the right and that he'd no doubt be facing a lot of jail time. He thought long and hard about that, rubbing his arms to try to stay warm in the cold room while he waited for the agent to return. After thinking some more, he got up and started pacing the floor.

The door creaked open a few minutes later, and the agent stepped back in, this time carrying a small satchel. "All right," he said, "let's get down to business." He pulled out a pen, a small pad, and a tape recorder and positioned them on the table in front of Prime. "I know you're smarter than the average thug, so we'll make this quick and simple. Just to let you know, all of this is done in totally confidentiality. Whatever we discuss between these four walls will stay between us."

Prime nodded his head in agreement. "Okay," he said flatly.

The agent looked at Prime, picked up his pen, then pressed the record button on the tape recorder. "Now, let's start with your supplier," he said, with his pen positioned, ready to write.

Prime inhaled deeply, let out the air out, and stared at the agent. "His name is Michael," he said, giving the agent a serious look.

"Michael? Okay," the agent repeated, then scribbled it on the pad. "Last name?"

"Jackson," Prime said, then smiled deviously. "So maybe you oughtta beat it."

The agent looked at Prime with pure hatred in his eyes. He grabbed the pen and pad and threw them at Prime. "So you wanna fuckin' play, huh? Well, fuck you then! You better hope you've got a damn good lawyer," the man snapped as he got up from the table. "And by the way, you better make sure your lady has one, too, 'cause we found plenty of drugs in the house as well," he added as he opened the door and walked out.

A few minutes later, a jailer arrived at the door to escort Prime back to his cell.

"Can I get my phone call?" Prime asked the jailer as they

walked down the long corridor.

"No," the officer barked before he ushered Prime into his small cell and locked the door behind him.

Prime stood in the middle of the room, mad and frustrated. "Damn it," he said under his breath, cursing himself for stashing his drugs in the same place where he and I laid our heads. "Damn the Feds, damn Big…and damn me for being such a damn fool!"

CHAPTER 18

Fiz and Jarvis were waiting out front when I walked out of the jail. Thanks to a couple of calls by Jarvis, I'd been bonded out and was—at least for a little while—a free woman again.

"Girl, what in the hell's going on? We heard Prime's locked up, too, but he ain't got no bond," Fiz said, hugging me as Jarvis talked on his cell phone.

"What!? I knew something had to be wrong. Thank y'all for gettin' me out. I need to talk to Prime," I said as Jarvis ended his call.

"So what's going on? You okay?" He clipped his phone on his belt and adjusted his Gucci frames.

"I'm cool. Just glad to be outta that nasty jail. I really appreciate y'all bonding me out," I repeated as we walked to Fiz's Benz and climbed in.

"Jarvis had his lawyer friend look into Prime's situation. He doesn't know all the details, but it's pretty deep," Fiz said, bringing her engine to life.

"Yeah, the Feds are cracking down pretty hard on your boy. More than likely, they'll try to pressure you to talk, since your name is on the house deed. It'd be smart for him to just claim it all and push you out of the picture. Y'all need to get with your lawyer and get on this ASAP," Jarvis explained.

As I sat in the back seat of the Benz SUV, I was at a loss for words. It was all new to me, and I didn't know what to do. "I, uh…I'll get on it," I stuttered, feeling helpless and frustrated.

As soon as we turned the corner onto my street, I noticed a van and two official vehicles in my driveway.

"What the hell's going on now?" Fiz asked as we pulled up to the front of the house.

Before we could get out of her Benz, a Federal agent walked over. "Hello. I'm Alan Moss. May I help you?" he asked, giving all of us a onceover.

I looked at him and rolled my eyes. "No. The question is, can I help you? Why are y'all still at my house?" I said as I pushed my door open hard and climbed out.

The agent looked at me with a smirk on his face. "So you're the not-so-lucky owner of this fine piece of property, huh? Well, ma'am, I'm sorry to inform you that this house has been seized by the Federal Government, and that includes that beautiful BMW in the garage," he said as I rounded the SUV.

My heart dropped. "Seized! How y'all just gonna take my house and car?" I screamed, getting in his face and about to really lose my cool.

He dug in his pocket and handed me some papers explaining the seizure.

I couldn't believe they could just come in and take all we had. My eyes watered as I flipped through the documents.

"As you can see, we are entitled to seize this property

because it can be presumed and is evident that drug money was used to purchase these possessions. I can escort you in to get some clothes, but everything else is being inventoried and will remain in the possession of the Federal Government until investigations are complete."

I wiped the tears away as I looked up at the Federal agents taking property from the house in storage boxes, marked as evidence. "How y'all just gonna take my house?" I asked, still not understanding any of it. "What the hell am I supposed to do? I don't have anywhere to go, nowhere to stay! I don't care about these stupid papers or any of this legal shit. That's my house, and I'm gonna go in there, take a bath in *my* tub, and sleep in my own damn bed!" I screamed as I stormed up the driveway.

Agent Moss quickly stepped in front of me, blocking my path. "Sorry, ma'am, but I can't let you enter without an escort," he said firmly.

I balled up my hands and looked at him, wanting to knock him out. "Get the hell outta my way!" I yelled as I tried to walk around him.

He reached around and pulled his cuffs from the small of his back, letting me know he would use them on me if I tried to enter my own home.

Just as I was about to make his ass haul mine back to jail, I felt a hand on my shoulder.

"Come on, Nikki. Just calm down. You're just gonna make it worse if you don't do as they say. You can stay at my place till you get all this worked out," Fiz said.

Meanwhile, Jarvis stood next to the SUV, talking to one of the other agents.

I looked up at Agent Moss and rolled my eyes. "You said something about getting some clothes. Can I at least do that now?" I asked, feeling helpless and alone without Prime there to make it better like he always did.

"As I said, I can escort you in for clothing. You may not remove anything else from the premises, and everything you do take with you will be inspected," he instructed coldly as he led me up to the house.

I kept my cool and bit my lip, even though I really just wanted to break down and cry. I felt so bad walking through my own shit, not able to touch anything or stay.

When I grabbed my toothbrush and deodorant from the counter, he barked, "Only clothing, ma'am," watching me like a hawk.

I growled and threw the items across the room. I snatched a couple outfits from the closet and stormed out with him hot on my heels. I didn't even look back as I walked out of the house.

Fiz and Jarvis were sitting in the Benz SUV waiting for me as I crossed the yard.

"Damn them," I muttered under my breath as I got in the back seat and threw my clothes down.

"It'll be all right, girl," Fiz tried to console me.

"I talked to one of the agents out there," Jarvis said. "Somebody fingered your man, more than likely someone who was trying to save his own ass," Jarvis said.

Fiz glanced at me in the rearview mirror, and we both shook our heads at each other before she pulled off.

CHAPTER 19

A week later, I'd finally had a chance to speak with Prime, after I'd written him a letter and included Fiz's number for him to call. We both knew he would need the proper representation if he was going to get out of jail. I had reached out to a couple of lawyers, and the best of the two wanted $150,000 to handle the case. I'd already run through the remainder of the money I had, and I was broke and relying on Fiz, who'd convinced me to join her at Shakers. Jarvis had stayed a few days before he had to jet back to Miami, leaving me a couple thousand that I promised to pay back.

"Girl, you gonna be just fine. Just follow my lead," Fiz told me as we entered Shakers for my first night on the job.

I had tried to find work to raise the $150,000 we needed for the attorney, and I knew a regular 9:00-to-5:00 wasn't going to cut it. Prime's court date was only twenty-eight days away, and if the attorney wasn't paid, he would be appointed a public defender; if that happened, we all knew he'd be up a creek without a paddle. I refused to let my man be railroaded, and one way or another, I was going to get whatever he needed. I was all Prime had, and I wasn't about to let him down, even if I had to shake my ass for a bunch of fat, horny strangers.

As we made our way through the club, men and women catcalled and whistled, trying to get our attention. I acted like I didn't hear them, but they grew louder and louder as Fiz made sure she acknowledged the crowd.

"Girl, if you plan on making the money to get Prime that fancy lawyer, you're gonna have to loosen up and do what you gotta do," she said as we stepped into the dressing room, where all the girls were stripping off their clothes in exchange for heels, thongs, and skimpy bikinis or no clothes altogether.

"I know. I'm just kinda nervous. I've never done anything like this. But you're right. I gotta get Prime that money," I said, dropping my bag to the floor.

"That's what's up! Come on, girl. Let's get it then!" Fiz said, stripping out of her clothes and squeezing into an outfit that didn't cover much of anything.

I followed her lead and did the same, dressing in the outfit we'd bought at the mall earlier. I glanced in the mirror and realized I really was one of the baddest bitches in the place. I checked myself out in the full-length mirror again, looking from head to toe before I walked out. I moved to the side so Fiz could give herself a quick inspection also.

"Showtime!" she called, then led the way from the dressing room out to the club floor.

The club was packed, and money was being thrown around like it grew on trees. I had a strange, euphoric feeling as I walked around, watching the naked and barely clothed women moving their bodies seductively for the strange men and women who were constantly tucking money into their g-strings and the straps of their heels.

"Say, shawty, over here! Let a nigga get a dance," a rough-looking man said as I walked by. He was sporting long braids and big jewelry.

I looked at Fiz questioningly, and she nudged me over in the direction of the man.

"It's your first dance, girl! Look at the bling on that boy! Go do your thang." She smiled and walked over to a group of young hustlers throwing money.

I walked over to the man and put my half-naked body in his face.

"Damn, baby, what's your name? You must be new," the roughneck asked.

I started moving to the beat of the music blasting from the sound system. "My name's Honey, and there ain't nothin' new about me," I said playfully, then turned around and showed him my ass.

He pulled a wad of money from his pocket and set it in his lap. "I hear ya, shawty, but ain't you, uh…gonna take all that shit off?" he asked, raising his eyebrows and smiling at me.

I looked around and saw that the other girls who were giving private dances were completely naked, so I played it off. "Damn, baby. Somebody's in a rush tonight. No foreplay or nothin', huh?" I said seductively, then stopped dancing and pulled off my top and bottom. It felt odd to expose myself to a sweaty stranger for money when the man I truly loved and respected was sitting in a cell, but I knew he was counting on me to get the money for a good lawyer. As I thought about Prime, I dismissed my feelings of guilt and embarrassment and just did what I had to do.

"Foreplay, huh? I like that," the roughneck said in a heavy

Southern drawl.

I showed him my most private parts, and he leaned back in his chair and started tossing bills at me.

After the song ended, he requested another dance and then another.

"Selfish boy," I said, facing him and putting my pussy in his face.

"Only when it comes to somethin' I really like," he said. "What would it take for us to spend a li'l time together somewhere more, uh...private?" he asked, licking his lips and looking me up and down like a Rottweiler staring at a steak.

I turned around and made my ass jiggle to the beat as I looked back at him. "We're already spending time, sexy," I replied, turning back to face him.

He shook his head. "Nah, beautiful, I mean time alone, just me and you. I'll make it well worth your while," he said as he picked up the stack of money off his lap.

I looked at the money and knew it had to be close to $8,000, a good start toward the $150,000 for the attorney fees, but then I dismissed the thought. "Sorry, boo. I don't get down like that," I said, smiling.

It seemed as if his whole demeanor changed when I declined to sell him my goods. He stood up, peeled off a couple of bills, then stuffed the rest back in his pocket. "I gotta respect that. You have a good night," he said, ending our dance session making it clear that if I wasn't selling, he wasn't interested.

I sucked my teeth, put my outfit back on, then went looking for the next horny nigga who was ready to lust over tits and ass. "Want a dance?" I asked an older, well-dressed, professional-looking man who looked totally out of place in Shakers.

"Why not?" he replied, moving his chair so I'd have room

NIKKI

to dance.

Just as I was getting naked, Fiz walked up to me, fully dressed. "Girl, I'll be back," she whispered in my ear.

I leaned in close to her. "Where you goin'?" I asked, looking over her shoulder at the good-looking brother who was standing behind her.

She turned and motioned to him. "'Bout to get this $3,000. Gotta get it how you live, girl! Jarvis be looking out, but ain't nothing like having your own. Ya feel me? You better get with the program, girl, 'cause just shaking your ass ain't gonna net you that $150,000 you need." With that, she winked, then turned and walked off with the handsome gentleman.

I turned my attention back to the older gentleman, who paid me in advance for two dances. As soon as I finished dancing for him, I quickly put on my clothes and rushed through the club, looking for the roughneck with the wad of money.

From that night on, there was a price on my time, and I didn't come cheap. I did it all for the love of my boo, Prime, and his lingering freedom. I wasn't sure if he would condone it, but I had to get him out.

CHAPTER 20

Two black vans rounded the corner and whipped behind the building that was once home to Mystic, a five-star restaurant that had been abandoned years ago, after the owners were murdered during a robbery. The two vans parked side by side and waited. A few minutes later, a white Maybach S57 pulled up with a U-Haul truck behind it. The man in the Maybach got out, spoke to the occupants of the vans in Spanish, then opened each van up and examined the contents. After checking out the cargo, he signaled the two men in the U-Haul over. He then got back in the Maybach and made a call. The two men from the U-Haul hurriedly moved the contents of the van into the back of their truck. By the time the Maybach was halfway to its next destination, the truck was pulling out from behind the restaurant with 250 kilos of cocaine in it.

"Ken Burns, my man, what will it be today?" Jarvis sat comfortably in the back of his Maybach as it cruised through downtown Miami.

"J-man, you know what it is, $25,000, fresh off the truck,"

Ken replied as he sat in the back office of his upscale clothing store, counting up the money for his next order.

"You clearing your whole tab today, right?" Jarvis asked as he thought about the $50,000 Ken had shorted him on the last buy and how he'd pretended it was a mistake.

Jarvis had long ago stopped counting Ken's money because they went way back and were good friends. Jarvis had been feeling some kind of way lately, though, because Ken was supposed to pay him a while ago but had been avoiding him. Now that he needed more product, he'd picked up the phone to return all of Jarvis's numerous calls.

"Yeah, uh…I'll clear up half now and the rest on the next one. Shit's been crazy around here, bruh. You know I got you though," Ken said as he wiped beads of sweat from his forehead.

Jarvis held his anger as the Maybach pulled up out front of his luxurious million-dollar, beachfront home, one of his many properties in Miami. "No problem. Half will be good," Jarvis said as his driver eased the custom car into the five-car garage.

"A'ight, bruh. You know I got you," Ken said as he played with the lines of cocaine he had laid out on the glass desk in front of him.

"That's cool. I'll have Zo stop by your spot. You there now?" Jarvis asked, stepping out of the car and heading into the house.

"Yeah, I'll be here for a couple hours," Ken replied. He then covered the phone and took a big drag, clearing the desk of one of the fat lines of coke.

"Okay. He's on the way," Jarvis said, kicking back on the bed and taking off his Mauri gators.

Before he could call Zo, his phone rang.

"Yeah?" he answered, recognizing the number of one of his U-Haul drivers.

"Everything is secure," the man said as they pulled away from Jarvis's motorcycle dealership that he used to warehouse his shipments.

"Okay. I'll be in touch." Jarvis clicked off the line then called Zo.

Zo picked up on the first ring. "Boss, what it do?" Zo asked as he pulled out of the McDonald's drive-thru, ready to satisfy his munchies after smoking a joint.

"I need you to head out to Ken's and show 'im a li'l love. Hit me when you leave," Jarvis ordered as he pulled off his button-down shirt and slacks and replaced them with a t-shirt and jeans.

"Okay. I'm on it," Zo said before he took a huge bite out of his Quarter Pounder.

* * * * *

Ken sat at his desk, counting the money up again and inhaling a couple more lines of the coke. He'd started getting high off his own supply, and his bad habit was causing him to do bad business, even going so far as to short his own workers. He'd sworn off the drug on many occasions but always ended up with his face on the table again, nursing another line, a slave to the drug that had earned him millions. He was sitting at his desk, all geeked up, when a knock at the door caught his attention. He jumped up, wiped the cocaine residue from his nose with a napkin, and headed to the front.

Zo stood on the other side of the door with a large canvas bag in his hands.

Ken turned the lock. "My boy Zo! What's happenin', playa?" he called out. He slapped Zo on the back, then closed the door behind him.

Ken and Zo had been meeting for buys for years and had grown close. In many ways, Zo thought of Ken as the big brother he'd never had. Ken gave Zo game every time he came through to do business, and he schooled him on the regular. Despite Ken's drug addiction, he was a real player and knew all the tricks of the trade. Over the years, he'd seen his young protégé rise through the ranks, and that made him very proud.

"I'm holding it down, man. What's up with you?" Zo asked as they made their way to the back.

"Ain't shit popping. Same old thang. Just another day, another dollar." Ken wiped his nose unconsciously as he rounded his desk.

Zo laid the large canvass bag on the desk next to the stacks of money for the buy.

"The street's are talkin', bruh. Whatever you're doin', it's caught up with you," Zo spat as he looked intently at the man he respected and admired.

Ken glanced up at Zo with a confused look on his face. "What you talking about, man? What do you mean?" he asked, trying to hide his guilt from his protégé.

"Open the bag," Zo said, pushing it closer to him.

Ken grabbed the bag, unzipped it, and pulled it open. His eyes widened when he saw nothing but a bunch of old newspapers. "Wh-what the fuck is this all about?" he asked as he picked up the bag and dumped the newspapers on the desk, looking for dope that wasn't there. When he glanced back up again, he was looking into the barrel of Zo's .40 caliber. "Zo, what's up, my brother?" Ken asked shakily as he locked eyes with Zo.

"I was sent here to kill you, to make your body disappear. You've been doin' a lotta bad business, my nigga, and on top of that, you've been using Jarvis's good name to cover your ass. He sent me to get rid of you," Zo said, tightening the grip on the gun.

"Zo, man, please don't play it like this, man. Listen, li'l bruh, I—" Ken started but was quickly cut off.

"Man, just disappear. Give me your word that you'll leave and that you won't ever come back. You're through here in Miami. Shit, you're through in the South period. Go up north, my nigga, 'cause you're a marked man. You gotta give me your word that you'll leave." Zo looked sadly at his old friend, whose appearance had changed over the months, and he tucked his gun back in his waistband.

"My word, man. I'm out," Ken said, wiping sweat from his nose with the back of his hand.

"Get outta town now, bruh," Zo said with authority.

"Okay, man. I got you," Ken said, grabbing the money off the desk and stuffing it in the bag.

After he finished, Zo reached out and stopped him. "That goes with me. Jarvis is gonna be looking for the money for the buy. If you wanna live, I've gotta turn this in to him." Zo reached over and grabbed the bag out of Ken's grip.

"Okay. A'ight, man. I got you," Ken said, grabbing his jacket and keys. He knew there was no use in closing up the store or going back to his house. If Jarvis wanted him dead, he wouldn't be safe anywhere in the South. *If I wanna live another day—or shit, even another hour—I better get the hell outta Dodge,* his mind warned him, reminding him of just how close Zo's gun had been to his face.

"You know how to reach me if you need me. Take care of yourself, man," Zo said, turning to exit the store with the bag of money.

Outside, Zo placed the money in the trunk of the car, then got in and pulled out of the lot. Before he turned into traffic, he picked up his cell and made a call. "It's done," he lied to Jarvis.

On his balcony, where he was smoking a Cuban cigar, sipping on a margarita, and watching bikini-clad women as they frolicked in the water and sunbathed on the beach, Jarvis smiled. "Good job," he said naïvely. "I knew I could count on you."

CHAPTER 21

"**P**rime, baby, I miss you so much." I was so happy to hear Prime's voice that I couldn't stop smiling. Two weeks had passed since I'd last heard from him, and his court date was exactly twelve days away.

"I miss you, too, baby. How are things coming along with getting the lawyer's money?" he asked in a concerned tone.

"Well, I've got $90,000 so far. I called the lawyer, and I'm meeting with him before the week's out. Baby, don't worry. I'll have all of it before it's time for you to go to court. I promise," I said, hoping he wouldn't question where the money was coming from.

"Boo, where you getting all that dough from? And did you holla at them folks like I told you to?" he asked.

I didn't want to tell him that the friends he'd told me to contact had stopped all contact with me after I'd told them he was locked up, so I brushed the question off. "Look, baby, don't worry about what's going on out here. You know I got you. Are you holding up okay in there? When can I come to see you?" I asked, hearing a lot of commotion in the background.

"I'm cool, baby—just waiting for this court date. I claimed all that shit in the house, Nikki. There ain't no way I'd ever let you take a fall. You just make sure you get the money from them niggas I told you to call. Which one you done got something from already?" he asked, forcing me to let him in on his so-called friends.

"Um…" I stuttered, not wanting to piss him off or dash his hopes. "Baby, it don't matter. Just—" I was cut off by the automated recording.

"You have thirty seconds," the operator said, letting us know his call for the week was about to end.

"Damn! Baby, I got you! Love you," I said, and my eyes began to water when the line went dead just as he was about to say something.

It had only been a little over two weeks, but I was knee deep in the stripping game. I took heed when Fiz told me that stripping alone wasn't going to earn the $150,000 for the lawyer in the amount of time I had. So far, I'd been on five dates, three of them repeats, and I was totally surprised at how easily the so-called ballers and players freely gave up their hard-earned gains for a quickie. It took me a while to get used to it, but I put my feelings to the side and did what I had to do to save my man.

I heard Fiz come in as I lay across my bed, flipping through the channels on the TV.

"Hey, girl. What up?" she said, dropping her Neiman Marcus bag in the chair.

"Shit, just chillin'. I see you still spending all that nigga's money," I joked, getting off the bed and grabbing her bag to see what she'd bought.

She tried to slap my hand away but was too slow. "Meh, if I

don't spend it, the next bitch will." She laughed as she plopped down on the sofa.

"Girl, this is nice!" I said, checking out her new Birkin bag. I turned the receipt over to see how much it cost.

"Damn, bitch, don't be checking my pockets," she said playfully, trying to grab the receipt from me.

I dodged her and saw that the bag cost $3700. "Shit! You're a master gold-digger!" I joked, giving her a high-five for getting a nigga to drop that kind of dough on her.

"School's in session for a small fee. Just let me know," she replied with sass in her tone, grabbing the bag from me.

"Whatever. I graduated my first week. I'm past good, Miss Thang," I said as I reached up under the bed and pulled out a shoebox.

"Pssh. Girl, you're just a rookie. I'm the vet here, so you best bow down." She raised her hand up and down, as if she was some kind of royalty.

I opened the shoebox and pulled the money out. "I make it rain though! Now who's the rookie?" I called out as I tossed the $96,000 playfully in the air.

She did a little dance in the shower of bills. "Oh shit! Prime's about to come home!" she said, doing a quick booty-pop to end her dance.

I smiled as I pictured him walking out of the Federal holding jail. "Yeah, my baby's comin' home," I said as I picked up all the lawyer's money and put it back in the box.

"I guess you ain't a rookie no more then. Just be careful, girl, and always make them niggas strap up," she advised me in a concerned tone.

I looked at her in disbelief; there was no way in the world I would let anybody but Prime penetrate me without protection, no matter how much money was on the table. "Come on now. You know I'm on point, girl," I replied, seeing the concern in her face.

"Yeah. Well, I'm heading in a li'l early tonight so I can catch my Asian money man. This muthafucker kicks close to a stack to blow in a bitch's pussy all night, some real freaky shit. I'll holla at you when you get there," she said, then left for the club and closed the door behind her.

I lay around flipping the TV. Just as I settled on *The First 48*, my cell phone rang. "Hello?" I answered hesitantly, as I didn't recognize the number.

"Hey, Nikki. Where's Fiz? I've been calling her number for a couple days now, but she hasn't returned my calls," Jarvis asked.

I was surprised he even had my number. I didn't know what to tell him, so I tiptoed around his question without giving him any specifics. "Hmm. I ain't talked to her or been at the house, but when I head in tonight, I'll let her know you're trying to catch up with her. I remember her saying she was having trouble with her phone, but I don't know if she got it fixed or not. Uh…not to sound rude or anything, Jarvis, but how'd you get my number?" I asked curiously.

"Fiz called me from your number a couple times, and I saved it. If it's a problem, I'll happily delete you from my contacts," he said with firmness in his tone.

"No, no it's cool. I don't mind. I'm gonna lock yours in just in case. When I get back in, I'll tell her you called," I said, trying to keep the awkward conversation short.

"Okay. I appreciate it. Have a good night," he said, ending the call.

I watched a few more episodes of *The First 48*, then got

up and got ready for work. I tried three times to call Fiz, but she didn't answer, so I assumed she was just out on the floor, soliciting dances.

My phone rang as I ran water in the tub. "Hello?"

"Hey, girl. I see you called. You good?"

"Yeah, I'm straight, but Jarvis called me earlier looking for you. I didn't know what to tell him so I said I haven't been home. What's going on, girl?" I asked, checking the temperature of my bath water.

"Look, I'ma take you to school one more time, but this time you're paying me. Didn't I say you're a rookie? When you got a man's nose wide open, you gotta fall back from time to time to keep him on his toes, which will keep him on his job. He's gonna miss you so much that when you finally grace him with your presence, he'll go all out to try to make you stay around. The way these niggas try to keep you from going ghost on 'em is to spend a lot on you, girl. So there's your lesson for the day. Always remember to put 'em on ice every now and then," she said with a laugh. "That's why I been freezin' Jarvis's ass for a while now."

"Whatever. Bye, Fiz!" I laughed it off but took heed to her words.

As I lay in the tub, letting the bubbles and warm water soothe me, thoughts of Prime invaded my mind. I said a silent prayer as I lathered up and rinsed off.

*****

"Girl, that nigga got it for real! I don't know where he been, 'cause he used to fall through here every week," Fiz said as she watched the man walk into Shakers, a fat black brother dressed in Gucci from head to toe.

I could tell he was somebody by the way the other hustlers and players in the club dapped him up, making it their business to greet the big man. "Oh yeah?" I asked as I watched him make his way to the VIP.

"Girl, that nigga spend good. I'm talking stacks on top of stacks," Fiz emphasized, staring as the big man made his way through the crowd.

"So, um…why ain't you milking that?" I asked, surprised at my own words. I was getting more used to the lifestyle than I even realized. Fiz wasn't one to let an easy dollar pass by, so it didn't make sense that she wasn't going after him.

"When I found out he knew Jarvis, I backed up. Damn if I'm gonna be all greedy and shit. Girl, he spend good money though. He used to fuck with Red Velvet, but that stupid bitch tried to go in the nigga's pocket while he was asleep, and he caught her ass. She tried her best to hide the black eye he gave her, but we all saw it. Ever since then, he's just been floatin' around," she said, turning her attention to a group of heavily jeweled, tall brothers who looked like basketball players.

By the time she turned back around, I was already heading across the floor to the VIP.

The big man zeroed in on my thick thighs and wide hips as I climbed the steps.

"You want a dance?" I asked, sashaying up and getting right in his face. I could tell my aggressiveness caught him totally off guard.

"Damn, shawty, it don't look like you gon' let me say no. Waitress, get me a bottle of Cîroc and two glasses," he said, then slowly eased his big body down on the sofa.

I looked over and saw a couple of the other dancers scoping

out the VIP, so I didn't waste time in getting naked. I knew
after he got an eyeful of my thick thighs, fat ass, and clean-
shaven lips, it'd be a wrap. "You're right. I don't know what
no means," I said. Determined to get the rest of the money for
my lover's lawyer, I dropped down low and spread my ass so
he could get a good look at my pussy from the back.

"Damn, baby," he said. Without taking his eyes off me, he
began rubbing his hands down the front of his pants.

I looked in his eyes and moved slowly in a snake-like
motion. "You like what you see?" I asked seductively as I
rocked back and forth, gyrating to the beat.

"Fuck yeah." He looked at me like he wanted to eat me up.

"I'm glad. Now touch it and see how soft it is." I tooted my
ass out and looked back at him.

He reached over and ran his stubby, fat hands over my ass,
then squeezed both my cheeks lightly. "Yeah, ma, you got
it goin' on. How 'bout you take the rest of the night off and
come wit' me?" he said just as the waitress arrived with the
two glasses and bottle of Cîroc.

I turned and faced him, still moving slowly to the beat. "If
I leave with you, I won't make my $500-plus quota for the
night," I said, placing my hands on knees and making my
cheeks jump.

"Your quota? You ain't gotta worry 'bout that. You gon'
make way more than any $500 fuckin' wit' me, baby," he said,
filling the two glasses with Cîroc.

"Oh yeah? Well, if you mean what you say, I'm game." I
stopped dancing and looked at him seriously.

He returned my gaze and took a big swallow of his drink.
"Money has never been an issue with me," he said as he
handed me the other glass.

I took a light sip. "Yeah, I heard you're big time. Ready when you are," I said, then took another sip.

A few minutes later, we were exiting the club. He opened the door of his smoke-gray BMW 760 to let me in.

"Don't wanna sound fucked up, but I gotta have my quota before I leave...and it'd be good if I knew your name," I said, buckling my seatbelt.

"My name is Booney. What's yours?" he asked as he dug in his pocket and pulled out a stack of bills.

"I'm Angel," I replied, watching him count out the bills.

"Here ya go. This oughtta cover your quota and then some," he said. He folded up the bills and handed them to me, $2,000, far more than my quota. Before we pulled off, he fished around under his seat and pulled out a plastic bag. "You fuck with the Mollies?" he asked, holding up a bag that contained eight pills.

I thought for a quick second before I answered. "Yeah," I lied, knowing I could sell them in the club later. He handed me the whole bag, and I tucked them in my clutch.

We pulled out and headed to his quarter-million-dollar condo in downtown Atlanta. We pulled into his parking garage ten minutes later. I didn't waste any time with the small talk as we entered his expensively furnished pad. A few minutes later, we were butt-ass naked in his bed, fucking like dogs in heat—or at least he was.

"Oh yes! Fuck this pussy!" I called out, putting on the best act in the world, not at all physically affected or impressed by his tiny manhood.

"Give Big Daddy that pussy! Shit yeah, bitch! Fuck Big Daddy, bitch!" he screamed as if he'd lost his mind.

I used my pussy muscles to milk his miniature package, ready to get it over with. "Oh, baby, I'm 'bout to nut! Nut wit' me!" I moaned, hoping he'd follow my lead; the 300 pounds of sweaty blubber were making me sick to my stomach.

"Here I come, bitch!" He panted hard as he sped up his pace.

I was about to lose it. I was really having a problem with him calling me a bitch, but I held my tongue as he started to shake and shiver. "Oh I'm cumming, too, Big Daddy!" I lied, grabbing a handful of his fat rolls and pinching him hard, intentionally trying to hurt him for calling me names.

"Mmm...fuck yeah!" he yelled as his body jerked.

"Oh yes," I chimed in as he rolled off me onto the soft California King mattress.

A little over ten minutes later, I was being dropped off at the club again, let out of the car without so much as a "Goodbye" or "Talk to you later." I didn't give a fuck, though, because I'd just made a quick $2,000 to put toward the lawyer's fees.

CHAPTER 22

B *leep! Bleep!*

The ringer rang twice, signaling that someone was entering or exiting. I lifted my head off the pillow, looked over at the bedside clock, and saw that it was almost 4:30 in the morning. Fiz had come in with me when we'd left the club around 3:00, so I figured something had come up and she'd left out without me hearing. All my assumptions went out the door when I looked up and focused on the masked man standing in the middle of my bedroom floor, holding a big black pistol.

"Don't fuckin' move. You scream, and I'ma kill your mutha-fuckin' ass," he growled as he stepped into my room and pulled the door closed behind him.

I sat there, speechless, looking at the man's single gold tooth in the bottom of his mouth. My whole body started to shake uncontrollably. "Please just get what you want and leave. I got money over there on the dresser, almost $3,000. Please don't shoot, man! That's all I got." As I pleaded with him for my life, flashbacks of my parents' senseless murder crossed my mind.

The man grabbed the money I'd made from tips and off Booney and stuffed it in the cargo pockets of his black fatigues. I knew Fiz was most likely knocked out cold from the long night at the club, so there was no point in hoping that she would save me. The man did a quick scan of the room, then started searching more intensely.

"Don't make a fuckin sound," he whispered, pausing to point the gun at me. When he was sure I'd be quiet, he started searching again.

The first place he looked was under the bed. I was glad I'd emptied the shoebox and hidden the money inside the lining of my old, raggedy leather jacket that hung in the back of the closet.

He grabbed the shoebox and opened it. When he saw that it was empty, he was instantly angry. "Where's the rest of the money? I ain't playing wit' yo' ass either!" he said with rage in his voice.

My heart dropped. The only other person who knew I had money in the shoebox was Fiz. I thought about that for a minute as the man waved the gun around. I refused to believe that my girl would sell me out, but I wasn't sure what else to think. "That's all I have. I swear! Please!" I cried out loudly, hoping Fiz would wake up and interrupt the man's mission.

"Shut the fuck up!" he spewed, sticking the gun directly in my face. He started frantically searching the room, and after coming up empty, he snatched the blinds from the window and used the cord to tie my wrists and ankles. Heated, he stormed out of my room and closed the door behind me.

I silently prayed as I lay across the bed, trying to free myself.

Nikki

"Hey!" he spat, nudging Fiz with the gun, trying to wake her.

Fiz brushed him off sleepily, unaware that the man was in her bedroom.

"Say!" he said, the pulled the covers off of her.

Finally awake, she took one look at him and jumped up. "What the hell, Cutty!? What you doin' in my room? Damn, nigga, this ain't part of the plan! Shit, you're supposed to be grabbing the money and getting the hell out!" she snapped.

"There ain't no money to grab! The bitch don't got nothin' but $3,000. You got me all up in this muthafucker, and there ain't shit to take." He sneered, pulling the hot mask off his face to get some air.

"Nigga, I told you it's in the shoebox under the bed," Fiz whispered.

"No the fuck it ain't! I already looked. I got the bitch tied up in there. This is what we're gonna do," he said, then rambled off his plan. Once Fiz was well informed, Cutty pulled the mask back down over his face, then went into action.

* * * * *

"Pleaseeee noooo!" Fiz yelled from outside my door.

I looked up as my room door opened, only to see the masked man dragging Fiz into my room by her hair.

"I'm killing both of y'all hoes if I don't have all the money from this spot in five seconds!" he said angrily, waving the gun around. He jerked Fiz around by her hair and roughly dragged her through the room.

G Street Chronicles / 137

"Nikki, just give him the money! He's gonna kill us!" Fiz cried, with tears running down her face.

The man then slapped her, sending her into the wall. After seeing him do all that to her, all my thoughts that she was behind it went out the window.

"Stop! Okay! Please just let us go. The money is in my black leather jacket in the back of the closet," I cried.

The man snatched Fiz up by her neck and threw her over to the bed next to me. "Bitch, don't move." He rushed over to the closet and grabbed the jacket. After making sure the money was inside it, he tucked it under his arm and made his way to the door.

Seconds later, the beeper on the front door sounded, letting us know someone had opened it.

"Call the police!" I screamed as Fiz untied me.

"No way, girl! I got pills and weed in there," Fiz said, helping me out of the cords.

"Fuck! So what do we do? God, why me?" I broke down in tears as I realized that all the lawyer's money was gone. I knew Prime didn't stand a chance without a lawyer, and he was counting on me to make that happen for him. I sat on the bed crying, trying to figure out what I was going to do. I refused to accept the fact that my man would be sent away for a long time just because I couldn't come through for him.

Fiz stopped pacing back and forth for a minute to hug me. "It's gonna be all right, Nikki," she said, all the while thinking about her cut of the $90,000 the man had just made off with.

"I know, sis, and I ain't about to give up on Prime," I said, more pissed off and determined than ever.

CHAPTER 23

"This is for you," Jarvis told Zo as they sat on his back balcony, enjoying the warm, salty breeze coming up off the beach.

"Thanks, fam', but what's it for?" Zo asked, looking down at the four kilos that sat in front of him on the table.

"For your loyalty and hard work. I've been busy and haven't had the chance to really thank you. Ya know, Zo, in our line of work, it's hard to find people we can really trust. When a man finds somebody like that, he's gotta let 'im know his value. This is on the house. Go sell it and splurge a little," Jarvis said, looking out over the glorious sunset on the horizon.

"Man, Jarvis, this ain't necessary. You already pay me good to do what I do," Zo said, now thinking twice about his decision to let Ken live. "I really appreciate ya, bruh."

"Just consider it a bonus. Speaking of what you do, though, did you properly dispose of the body? We don't need no unwanted attention later on," he said as he picked up his Cuban cigar and lit it.

"It's all taken care of. He'll never be found," he lied, then swallowed hard.

Jarvis took a long drag off the cigar, then laid it down in the crystal ashtray on the table. "There's something else."

"What is it, Boss?"

"I want to talk to you about moving up. You've proven yourself worthy, and I'm ready to give you more responsibility." Jarvis placed his hands on the rail and gazed out at the white, sandy beach gathering his thoughts.

"More responsibility? What you got in mind?" Zo asked, walking over standing next to Jarvis.

"I feel like you're ready to move up to the next level. You've put in the work and paid your dues, and now it's time that you start runnin' with the leaders of the pack...or do you think you need a li'l more prepping?" Jarvis asked, looking over at Zo with raised brows.

Zo looked Jarvis in his eyes and answered, "I'm ready for whatever you got for me. What do you have in mind?" Zo asked, trying his best to hide his excitement.

"I want to make you my lieutenant. You, of all people, know how I look at lieutenants in this game. I'll be trusting you with my life. You'll basically run the city as me. I'm gonna let all my contacts know that you'll be acting as me on all buys and sales, and I gotta trust that you won't abuse the authority I'm turning over to you," Jarvis said. He then walked back over to pick up his cigar and take another toke.

"Never, Boss," Zo replied sternly, then nodded to show his understanding of and agreement with what Jarvis was saying. Now he was regretting that he hadn't actually killed Ken; there was a great risk that the man might go against his weak word and resurface. If that happened, Jarvis would hold him responsible and come down on him with the ultimate punishment, a death sentence carried out in the streets. While Zo listened to Jarvis and tried to digest his words, he had a change of heart; he couldn't let Ken live after all. He would have to break his own word before Ken broke his.

"Do you agree?" Jarvis asked, leaning his head back to blow out a cloud of cigar smoke. "Totally…and you got my word that I'll never abuse the authority," Zo said with all sincerity.

"I trust you, man. Now get that illegal stuff off my property and go have yourself a good time. Call me tomorrow so we can hit the city hard and let everybody know you are now my second-in-command," Jarvis said as he dumped the cigar ashes over the rail.

"A'ight. I'll get at you tomorrow." Zo grabbed the kilos off the table and climbed down the back balcony steps, then rounded the house to his car.

Jarvis finished his cigar out on the balcony, then went in and called Fiz. The phone rang three times, then went to voicemail. He searched his contact list and made another call.

* * * * *

"Hello?" I answered, sitting on the couch, contemplating whether or not I should go to work.

Fiz had cut out earlier, after we'd sat around all morning, trying to figure out who was behind the robbery.

"Hey, Nikki, did you ever get with Fiz? Is everything okay?" he asked, interrupting my thoughts.

"We had a…well, a situation, and shit's kinda fucked up right now," I said, tearing up again as I thought about letting Prime down.

"A situation? What kind of a situation? Are y'all okay?" he asked, concerned.

"Well, we got robbed last night, and the man took all the money I'd saved up for Prime's lawyer. I can't believe this shit! He got everything." I sighed deeply before I spoke again. "I'm sorry, though, Jarvis. This isn't your problem. I'll make sure I tell Fiz you called," I said, wiping away more tears.

"Robbed? Somebody robbed y'all?" Jarvis asked, surprised. As far as he was concerned, we would have been the last target for a robber unless someone knew there was a large amount of money in the spot.

"Yeah. They got me for a li'l over $93,000, all the money I had for Prime's lawyer. After trying to piece it all together, all we can guess is that Fiz forgot to lock the door last night when we came home from the club. She was out of it and tired," I said, still wondering in the back of my mind if she was involved somehow.

"So Fiz left the door open and somebody came in and robbed y'all?" he asked, as if he also felt like something wasn't right.

"Yeah," I said, realizing how suspicious it sounded when he said it out loud like that.

"Who else knew y'all had that much cash stashed there?" he asked.

"Nobody but me and Fiz, far as I know," I answered dryly.

"You think Fiz had something to do with the robbery?" he asked.

"I-I really don't know. I hate to think so, but—"

"Nikki," he said, cutting me off, "girl, you know Fiz is my people, but scandalous shit from anybody don't sit well with me. I hope she isn't responsible for some low-down shit like that," he said in a serious tone.

"Yeah, I know." I exhaled.

"Where is she anyway?" he snapped.

"She left early to do something. I'm not sure where she went," I said, realizing that was strange; she usually always told me where she was going.

"I don't know what's up with her. She hasn't hit me up in a while, and that's not like her. She's been real distant lately, like she's up to something. When you see her again, tell her to call me ASAP. Meantime, is there anything I can do to help you out?" he asked.

I thought more and more about the night's events, right up to the moment when Fiz had refused to let me call the police. My mind was in a panic, desperate to find a way to replace the money in time for Prime's court date. I thought for another minute and then remembered that Prime had given me the numbers of some of his alleged friends. *He supplied them on the regular, so why can't I step into his shoes and do it?* I had ridden with him and watched him long enough to know how to handle the business, and I knew Jarvis could fill me in on anything else I needed to know. "You think you could front me some work?" I blurted out.

"Work? What do you mean by that?" he asked, confused.

I did some quick numbers in my head. "I'm thinking ten kilos. I know—"

He stopped me in a hurry. "I don't know what you're talking about when it comes to kilos, but I can help you with a job. I'm hiring at the shop. Let me know when you're ready, and I'll send for you."

It didn't take long for me to pick up on the fact that he was trying to steer the conversation away from certain topics on the phone. I knew then that I'd been reckless, and I paused, hoping I hadn't gone too far. "Oh, I…yeah, I'd love a job at the shop. When can I come down?" I asked, ready to make it happen.

"Do you have any references or prior experience? I'd hate for you to come down here and have no idea what to do," he said, speaking in codes I finally recognized.

"I've been well trained, and Prime's people can give me a reference if needed," I said, selling myself the best I could, hoping he'd help me out.

The line grew quiet, and I grew nervous waiting for his response. Finally, he answered in a firm tone, "Okay. I'll help you out with a job."

My heart skipped a beat. "Jarvis, can you, uh…keep this between us? I don't wanna feel like this, but I don't fully trust Fiz right now." Right after I made the remark, I peeked out the window to see if she'd gotten back.

"I totally understand. I'll call you once everything is situated. You good to leave today?" he asked, catching me off guard.

"Shit, I'm ready right now," I said excitedly, ready to do whatever I had to do to get my baby home.

"Okay. I'll get with you later. Just be on standby," he said, then ended the call.

I went to the back to find the numbers of Prime's friends, then rushed to get ready for my upcoming trip to Miami.

CHAPTER 24

"Shawty, you almost had me goin' ham up in that bitch," Cutty told Fiz as they sat in the kitchen of his one-bedroom apartment on the west side of the city.

"Man, I told you she was stackin'. But why the fuck did you pull my shit so hard? You slung me around the damn room like a ragdoll!" Fiz complained, swatting him on the arm.

Gabby walked by to go to the fridge. She gave them a blank stare as they sat at the table, splitting up the money from the robbery. Cutty looked up at Gabby as she cut her eyes in their direction, and then he went right back to dividing their take. Fiz rolled her eyes at Gabby as she walked back out.

Fiz and Cutty had been fucking around for a couple of weeks, and every time she came to the apartment, all she got from Gabby were mean mugs and frowns. Fiz and Cutty went way back and had known each other since high school; that was the only reason Fiz gave him a chance, considering he was a broke-ass tuna fish eater with caviar dreams.

Cutty had been one of the most popular guys at Banneker

High in College Park, but after graduation, when he entered the real world, he'd failed miserably. After dropping out of tech school, he'd tried his hand at drug dealing, which had netted him nothing but five years' probation. One night he made a pit stop at Shakers to have a couple drinks and was surprised to bump into his old classmate.

Fiz had had the biggest crush on Cutty back in the day when he was a young, brown-skinned pretty boy, so she was willing to overlook his light pockets and give him a chance. Since that night, she'd been looking out for her old flame on the regular, helping him out with tips and other money she came across. He was her dirty little secret, and she liked it that way. As soon as she'd seen Nikki's money in the shoebox, she'd instantly thought of Cutty and how easy it would be for the two of them to take it.

"What the fuck is her problem? Why is she always watching me like that? I know she's fam' and all, but she's about to make me show my ass up in here," Fiz snapped as Gabby slammed the bathroom door.

"Baby, just chill. You know she stay on the bullshit. You oughtta be used to that shit by now," Cutty told her, reaching over to rub her thigh. He knew Fiz made good money in the club, so he made it his business to make her his. He was well aware that Fiz only fucked with rich niggas who could afford all the luxuries of life, so he made sure he made it up to her whenever he got her into bed. He turned it up every time they had sex, fucking her like a porn star for hours. After their second night of mind-blowing sex, he'd accomplished his mission. He had Fiz's nose so wide open that she couldn't see the obvious.

"A'ight, but I'm trying my best to keep it ladylike up in here," Fiz said, leaning in, sticking her hands in his pants and grabbing his dick.

"Money first," Cutty joked. He grabbed her wrist and pulled her hand out, turning her focus back to the cash on the table.

Fiz was horny, though, and was more interested in dick than dead presidents. "Shit, baby, that money ain't goin' nowhere. Now give Mama her treat." She got out of her chair and straddled him.

"Baby, we got business to handle. I'll make it up to you tonight," Cutty said, trying to get Fiz out of his lap.

She acted as if she hadn't heard him. She leaned in and planted kisses on his ear and neck. She felt his dick getting rock hard as she wiggled around on it. She was dressed scantily in a red g-string under her sundress, which was now hiked up around her waist. "How 'bout a quickie?" She moaned as she pulled her g-string to the side and started pulling at his pants.

Cutty really wanted to fuck Fiz right then and there in the kitchen, but he knew if he tried some shit like that, Gabby would kill both of them. When Cutty first ran back into Fiz and saw that she was willing to look out for him in a major way, he put Gabby, his girlfriend and soon-to-be baby-mama, up on his plan. At first it was cool with her because her hair and nails, which hadn't been tended to in quite some time, were now getting done on the regular. Gabby was now keeping gas in her old Toyota and eating out from time to time, thanks to Fiz. She and Cutty had been struggling, so when Fiz came into the picture and she had to pretend she was just Cutty's cousin, it hadn't been a problem at first; it all seemed like a good trade-off for the money Fiz was bringing into their lives. Now that Fiz was coming over on the regular, though, a problem was exactly what it was becoming for Gabby.

"Baby, I gotta take care of some shit right quick," Cutty said.

But Fiz didn't move, not wanting to take no for an answer.

Cutty's heart skipped a beat when he heard Gabby coming back toward the front. Even though Gabby was going along with the plan, she had never witnessed him getting intimate with Fiz in any kind of way, something he told her didn't happen often. Gabby knew he was fucking Fiz but took his word that it had only happened twice and wouldn't happen again. Gabby wasn't slow by any means, and she knew there was no way in the hell that Fiz was giving Cutty all her hard-earned money without getting anything in return. Gabby had made her mind up to deal with it as long as the money kept rolling in and as long as it wasn't done around her.

"I can't hear youuuuu!" Fiz said playfully as she unbuckled his pants.

Gabby almost blew her top when she walked up and saw Fiz in Cutty's lap. She cleared her throat loudly, making both of them turn and look at her. "Hey, Cutty can I holla at you right quick?" Gabby asked snappily, standing in the doorway with a crazed look on her face.

"Yeah, a'ight. Excuse me, baby." Cutty lifted Fiz up off of him.

Fiz sucked her teeth and rolled her eyes as she watched Cutty follow Gabby out of the kitchen, stomping to the back. Seconds later, the bedroom door slammed. Fiz went and sat on the couch and flipped the TV on as she waited for him to return. *Why am I even dealing with this broke-ass nigga when I got men showering me with money on the regular, men like Jarvis?* She wondered that often, but then her thoughts always went back to the way Cutty sexed her and the phenomenal things he did with his tongue.

"Nigga, what the fuck was that all about? You straight up

disrespecting me in my own shit! You need to get that bitch outta here now, and I ain't fuckin' playin' wit' you, Cutty!" Gabby sneered, getting up in Cutty's face.

He grabbed her and took her in his arms. "Hold that shit down, baby. You know it ain't even like that. I gotta play the game to keep this ho kicking. You like your new outfits and shoes, don't you? All that good food we been eatin'? Them things you been able to buy for our child? We just hit for over $40,000, thanks to that bitch. Just chill, boo, till I can slowly fade her off," Cutty told Gabby as he held her by her wide hips.

"I ain't about to be all right with you and that bitch doing that shit all up in my face," Gabby said angrily, looking up at him.

"I got you, baby. Just chill out. I'm working on cutting it off since we straight now," he said, leaning in kissing her.

Gabby pulled away and flopped down on the bed as Cutty went back to the front with Fiz.

"I gotta take care of some shit. We'll get together later tonight," Cutty said, grabbing his share of the money off the table.

Fiz grabbed her purse and stood. "Yeah, whatever. Just call me," she said with attitude as she took her share and stuffed it in her purse.

"Baby, quit tripping. You know I'll make it up to you tonight," Cutty said while thinking of a way to get half of her cut.

Fiz walked up on him, gave him a deep, passionate kiss, then turned and walked to the door. "I'll hold you to it," she said.

Gabby watched them through the crack of the bedroom door, just seconds away from blowing the whole plan.

* * * * *

Fiz arrived back at the apartment later and found the letter I'd left on the bed, telling her I'd be gone for a couple days.

CHAPTER 25

I looked through the plane window at the palm trees and exotic birds as the plane descended into Miami International Airport. It was my first trip to The Sunshine State, and I could already see why it was a favorite vacation destination.

As I made my way through the airport, I spotted Jarvis standing next to the baggage claim, talking on his cell phone. "Hey, Jarvis!" I called out, causing him to turn around as I walked up behind him.

He turned with his phone still to his ear. "Nikki! What's up?" he acknowledged, then whispered something into his phone and ended the call.

"You tell me. I'm in your city," I said playfully as we made our way through the busy airport and out the double doors to the parking lot.

"Another day, another dollar. Ya feel me?" he said, handing me the keys to a big white Cadillac Escalade ESV rental.

"I see we're on the same page, but, uh…who's supposed to drive this big, pretty truck?" I asked, looking up at the sleek, chromed-out SUV.

He looked at me and smiled. "Sorry, but it was all they had available. Drive around and meet me up front. I'll be in a black Aston with black rims," he said, then made his way back across the lot and disappeared between the cars.

I pulled up behind him and pressed the horn once. A few minutes later, we were back to back, heading through downtown Miami, with him in the lead. The city landscape was just like what I'd seen in the movies: exotic birds, palm trees, beachfront homes, and scorching heat.

We pulled up into a section of the city called South Beach. After we rode by all the eateries and night spots, we came upon a cluster of million-dollar oceanfront mansions. We pulled up in front of the second house on the street, a multimillion dollar estate right on the white, sandy beach. I parked the truck behind him and got out.

"Nice place you got here, big baller," I joked as we headed up the driveway and into the house.

"Thanks," he said, not acknowledging my playfulness. He quickly dialed a number on his cell phone.

The house was like something straight off of *Lifestyles of the Rich and Famous*. The black and silver décor gave it a dark, futuristic feel. The place was immaculate, without a speck of dirt or dusk anywhere in sight; clearly he had a regular cleaning crew. All the large glass windows gave a grand view of the pearly white, beautiful beach.

"I'll have everything set for you in a minute. Where are the keys to the truck?"

I caught him discreetly checking me out from head to toe as I dug in my pocket for the keys. "I really appreciate you helping me out. I didn't know what I was gonna do," I said, thanking him again while looking around the lavish home.

"It's all good. Just tell me exactly what went on? What, exactly, do you think Fiz is into?" he asked as we took a seat across from each other on his soft, imported leather couches.

I ran my hand through my hair, then began to fill him in on the events of the night and her quick departure the next morning. After talking through and analyzing all the facts, we both came to the same conclusion, one I didn't want to believe.

"I felt it the whole time. I-I just can't believe her," I said, shaking my head.

The way he looked me straight in my eyes as he talked to me made me feel like a child talking to my father. His deep, firm voice only added to that feeling. "So are you gonna trust stayin' with her with all you're about to have going on now? It's going to be hard to hide this sort of thing when both of y'all are under the same roof," he said.

Ding-dong!

The doorbell interrupted our awkward and somewhat painful conversation about my best friend's betrayal.

"I'm not going to the apartment with it. I'll get a hotel room until it's all sold," I said as he got up to answer the door.

Jarvis opened the door and handed the keys to the truck to whoever was outside, then walked back over and sat across from me again. "A hotel would be your best bet. But what's going on with her otherwise? Why hasn't she returned my calls?" he asked, giving me a stern look, as if he dared me to lie and would know it if I did.

His cold stare had me shaken, making it hard for me to tell him anything but the truth. Besides that, Fiz had crossed me, but Jarvis, on the other hand, was helping me. "She's been getting your calls," I said bluntly, then paused.

He frowned and sat up on the edge of the couch.

"Then why hasn't she answered or called back?" he asked with a hint of anger in his tone.

I thought for a minute. *Fuck Fiz,* I finally said to myself. *That bitch stole my money, stole Prime's attorney's money.* "Probably because you're not her only significant other," I said with emphasis, purposely trying to make things bad for her.

He looked down at the floor, then back up at me. "I kinda figured she had a li'l young nigga on the side, but that's still not a reason to avoid my calls," he said, staring me down.

"She said she thinks you look out more for her on the money tip when she dodges you, and she's been dating other niggas, trying to get paid," I said, ratting her out. I didn't care anymore; she'd crossed me, even knowing my man's life was on the line, and I didn't care what happened to her.

Jarvis's facial expression finally changed, letting me know I'd gotten to him. "Oh yeah? So she's playing kid games with intentions of getting more money out of me? And she's fucking around with other men for money, like some kinda ho?" he asked with disgust in his tone.

I looked at him and nodded, making sure he was hanging on my every word. "Yeah, that's what she's up to. She fucks all kinds of big ballers for money. I'm sorry to tell you this, Jarvis, but you're not the only one lookin' out for her. She's got a whole buncha noses wide open," I said, not regretting a word of it.

"So that's why you called me a big baller when we arrived?" he said, breaking into a smile.

I laughed as the mood lightened. "Yeah, big baller!" I called out, making him laugh.

"I appreciate your honesty, Nikki. You want a drink?" he offered as he stood and walked over to the bar.

"Nah, I'm good. I gotta get on the road tonight," I said while he looked through the liquor.

"Not tonight. You'll be leaving in the morning, after everything is set. One drink ain't gonna hurt ya. I got a nice glass of Ace of Spades comin' right up," he insisted as he poured me a glass.

"I guess…if you insist." I examined the pretty crystal glass as he handed it to me.

He filled his glass, then took a sip. "Nikki, you're a damn beautiful woman, and you're so loyal to your man. I admire the extent you're willing to go to to help him get out of his current predicament. Any man would be lucky to have a woman like you," he said as we sat side by side on the couch in front of the large tropical fish tank that took up the whole far wall.

I tried my best to hide my blushing. "Thanks. I really appreciate you helping me help him. I want Prime to come home," I said, taking a sip from the glass.

"No problem. Have you eaten?" he asked gulping down the remaining contents of the glass.

"No…and I'm starving," I said, rubbing my hand across my stomach.

"Say no more. Let's go," he said, setting his glass on the table.

I set my glass down and stood, feeling a light tingle go through my body.

We exited the house, got in the Aston, and headed out to Casa Tua, an upscale restaurant Jarvis frequented. Fifteen minutes later, we pulled up, got out, and Jarvis passed his keys to the valet.

"Hi, Mr. Jarvis. Will you be expecting more company?" the tuxedo-clad host asked as we stood outside the dining area.

"No. It's just me and my lady friend here. Could you seat us in the garden area?" Jarvis requested, looking in the direction of the bistro seating.

"Very well, sir." The host nodded and led us across the floor, out to an elegantly decorated patio, decorated with tropical plants and flowers in a rainbow of vibrant colors.

I felt completely out of place in such a place, as I was just dressed in jeans and sneakers, and all the other diners were dressed extravagantly. "You should have told me to dress up," I said, scanning the crowd. "I'm dressed worse than the help!"

"I know you didn't have any proper attire in that small bag you brought. But don't worry, Nikki. Your natural beauty makes up for it. I'm sure you'd look stunning anything, and you fit right in," he said, looking at me with lust in his eyes, the same thirsty look I saw from the men at the club.

"Thanks," I said, suddenly feeling a little uncomfortable. A crazy sensation came over me, some kind of nasty mix of fear and guilt, and I wanted to leave. Looking across the table at Jarvis only made me more uncomfortable. I saw him as nothing more than a business partner, but the look in his eyes told me he was thinking something else entirely. I looked around for the waitress, hoping he would take our order so we could eat and run.

Finally, a server showed up at our table. "Hello. My name is Franco. What can I get for you?"

Jarvis ordered for both of us as I just sat there in a daze.

"Appetizers?" he asked, tucking the menus under his arm.

"No, that'll be all," Jarvis said, all the while keeping his eyes locked on me.

"All right. It'll be about ten minutes," Franco said, then walked off.

When the lamb chop dinners arrived, I dug in. I ate faster than I'd ever eaten before, in a hurry to end the so-called date, and I hoped Jarvis would do the same. I tried to stay cool and contain my uneasiness, because I really needed his help; he was Prime's only hope.

"That was delicious man, I'm full," I said, leaning back in my chair.

"Yeah…and that's why this is my favorite spot," he said, wiping his mouth with the napkin while looking for the waiter. "Time for dessert now," he said, waving Franco over.

"No, Jarvis, I can't eat another bite, and I got the –itis coming on," I said, ready to go.

"Come on now, Nikki. You gotta taste their famous cherry cheesecake. You can't eat at Casa Tua without ordering a slice," he insisted.

"I don't have the room," I said seriously.

He straight up ignored me and asked Franco, "Can you bring two cherry cheesecakes?" He looked at me and smiled seductively, really pushing me to the limit with his continuous thirsty looks.

"Jarvis, I appreciate it and all, but I have to get some sleep. I've got a long drive tomorrow and—" I started, trying my best not to offend him.

"So you're gonna be a spoilsport, huh?"

"Sorry," I said sheepishly."

"Cancel the desserts, Franco, and just bring me the check," Jarvis said, then reached over to pat my hand that was resting on the table.

I pulled my hand away and faked a girly giggle. I was ready to get the hell away from Jarvis because he was really creeping me out. It didn't take long for me to realize I'd pegged him all wrong; he was just as bad as some of the hard-up men who frequented the club. The only difference was that he had more money than most of them. "I really am sorry, Jarvis. There's just been a lot going on, and I really need some rest," I said as the waiter went for the check.

Ten minutes after we left the restaurant, we were pulling back in the driveway.

"Damn! I forgot my bag in the truck. Is there any way you can get it back for me?" I said, really frustrated.

"Not tonight, but I'll make sure you have it first thing in the morning," he replied, killing the engine.

I held my head to soothe the headache I could feel coming on. "Fuck. Could you just take me to my hotel room please?" I said, pouting. I laid my head back on the seat and closed my eyes.

He looked at me with a confused look on his face. "You don't have a hotel room. I already set up a guestroom for you for tonight. How in the hell could I put you up in a hotel when I have three extra rooms here that are unoccupied?" He pushed the door open and got out.

I didn't respond. I just let it go and got out behind him. As soon as we got in the house, he showed me to my room, and I hurried to lock the bedroom door and hop into bed.

Later that night, I was awakened out of my deep sleep by a knock on the guestroom door. "Yeah?" I answered groggily, wondering what he could possibly want at that hour.

I heard a key in the lock, then Jarvis opened the door and walked in. He walked over and looked down at me. "Mind if I join you?" he asked, opening up his robe and proudly displaying a pair of silk boxers, as if he was sure I wouldn't argue.

I sat up in bed and just looked at him, trying to find the right words to turn him down without blowing our business deal. "Jarvis, I…this isn't what we're all about. I got a man, and I think we oughtta keep it all business between us," I said calmly, really wanting to cuss his ass out.

"I figured you might wanna help me out, since I'm helpin' you—you know, return the favor and all," he said as the bulge in his boxers grew.

I thought about it for a minute and reflected back on all the other men I'd slept with to help Prime. On the flight to Miami, I'd decided to put that life behind me, assuming I would now have a way to make money without having to sell myself. Just when I thought all of that was over, I was being forced to deal with it again. I looked up at Jarvis, rolled my eyes, and slid over so he could get in. I refused to let Prime down, even if that meant helping other men get it up.

The next morning, I was on my way back to Atlanta in the big Cadillac ESV with ten kilos in the back, ready to hit the streets to get the money for my baby, just the way he'd taught me to.

CHAPTER 26

"**M**an, what the fuck are you still doin' in town? Bruh, you promised! I told you niggas are gunnin' for you!" Zo screamed into his cell phone at Ken while he headed to the Aventura Mall to meet him.

"We'll talk when you get here. Just chill, li'l bro," Ken said, riding in the passenger seat as his sidepiece, Kayla drove.

"Man, you fuckin' tripping, a'ight?" Zo slammed his phone down. He knew that if Jarvis caught wind that Ken was still living, he would more than likely become a marked man himself. He'd gone back and forth on his decision to let Ken live, but now he really regretted it. Now he had no choice but to kill the man himself.

As they rode down Third Street, he reached under his seat and pulled out his .45 Cobra. He cocked it and dropped it in the door compartment next to him. He turned into the mall parking lot and parked right outside of the food court doors to wait for Ken to show. A honking horn caught his attention. He turned in his seat and saw a woman behind the wheel of a new

Camry. Looking close, he spotted Ken hunched down in the passenger seat, trying to hide. They pulled off to the far side of the lot, and Ken got out and hopped in with Zo.

"Ken, what the fuck you up to? You gave me your word that you'd get outta town if I spared your ass. You need to stick to your word before someone else sticks you, man! I done told everybody you're dead, so you need to go before somebody sees you!" Zo yelled. He looked around at all the people and realized it wasn't right time to end Ken's existence.

"I know, I know," Ken said, wiping his face with the palm of his hand. "I've just got too much invested in this city to just up and leave. I reached out to one of my old friends, and he gave me a loan, enough to clear my face in the streets. I'm not gonna run from this shit, bruh. I'm gonna pay all these niggas and get right again," Ken said, darting his eyes around.

Zo wanted to grab his gun and take care of Ken once and for all, but he knew doing it in his car in a busy mall parking lot would surely get him locked up for a long time. Still, he had to do something to keep Ken from surfacing. He was now Jarvis's right-hand man, and he wasn't about to let Ken's sloppy ass fuck up that hard-earned promotion. "I'm gonna help you, man. Meet me tonight. I'll call and tell you when and where, 'cause we can't have you bumpin' into Jarvis or any of them other niggas you owe. Bruh, you got a huge-ass target on your head, and niggas trying to collect. What the hell you got on anyway?" Zo asked, noticing the bulge under Ken's shirt.

"Bulletproof vest. Gotta stay safe. I'm just gonna pay all these niggas, lie low for a minute, then slowly ease my way back into the game," Ken said, lifting his shirt to reveal the Kevlar. "Body Armor Threat Level IIIA, best vest on the market. This shit'll stop any handgun on the street," Ken boasted, then pulled his shirt back down.

"Interesting. But what if somebody aims for yo' head?" Zo asked, trying to make a valid point.

Ken swallowed hard, then looked around. "That's why I need to pay everybody off as soon as possible. I can't keep living like this, man, always lookin' over my damn shoulder." Beads of sweat began to form on his nose and forehead.

"That's what I'm tellin' you, bruh. That's why I'm gonna handle this shit for you. Don't go trying to connect with nobody. Just let me set it all up. I get together a meeting with the people who really matter, the ones who can kill all this bullshit," Zo said, knowing he had to make his move quickly if he was going to get rid of Ken.

"Man, you know I appreciate you. I'll just lie low and wait for you to hit me up." Ken looked around, pushed the car door open, then rushed back to the Camry, where Kayla sat waiting on him.

Zo grabbed his gun from the door compartment and checked the scene once more. He hit the horn and flagged Ken down before they could pull off. He looked around again, opened his door, and stepped out with his gun concealed under his shirt. Just as he walked up on the passenger side where Ken was sitting, a police cruiser pulled over to the side of the lot in their vicinity.

"Yo, what's up?" Ken asked as Zo got up to his window. "Forget somethin', man?"

Zo played it off. "Uh…just make sure you don't contact nobody till I get this shit straight. Be careful, Man," Zo said.

Ken gave him a confused look. "I know, bruh. You already told me that. I got you, man," Ken said, motioning to Kayla to pull off.

<u>Damn</u>, Zo thought, cutting his eyes over at the police cruiser that was parked just a few feet away from them. Zo turned and walked back to his car, knowing Ken had to be taken care of, sooner rather than later. *Why the hell did I let him go in the first place?* he scolded himself.

* * * * *

Later that evening, Ken and Kayla drove out to Wayne's crib. Wayne was the first one Ken called when he decided not to leave the city and to pay off all his debts instead. Ken and Wayne had been friends for years, and Wayne was very interested in buying into his old friend's businesses. He had watched Ken close all his other businesses after they'd stopped turning a profit, but the restaurant was still a big money earner.

Ken had walked into Wayne's office less than twenty-four hours ago asking to borrow $400,000, and he was willing to put the business up for collateral. Wayne quickly wrote up the papers and took control of the million-dollar establishment. Ken hated to do it, but he really had no choice if he wanted to stay alive and live in the South. When Wayne realized Ken had left one of the documents unsigned, he'd summoned him back to his office.

"Pull up to the mailbox," Ken told Kayla, opening his door to get out.

Wayne had dubbed his mansion "Wayne's World" because of its 11,000 square feet and the 4 acres it sat on.

"Hey, old friend! Come on in!" Wayne bellowed from the front door, noticing the beautiful woman Ken had with him.

"How's it going? This is my lady friend, Kayla," Ken introduced as they made their way across the marble floor of the foyer and into Wayne's office.

"Hi, Miss Kayla. I'm glad I am able to assist you and Ken," Wayne said slyly, knowing he'd taken advantage of the whole situation.

"Yeah…and we appreciate you," Ken said, a bit confused.

They stepped into the back office and waited as Wayne pulled all the paperwork from their deal out of the file cabinet. Wayne smile to himself, knowing the restaurant would be all his if Ken didn't pay him $600,000 in thirty days, which would be a large feat for him. He couldn't wait to own his old friend's establishment, one he knew he could easily expand and increase revenue.

"We forgot to sign these," he said, then paused long enough to glance up and see Kayla pointing a gun at him. "Um… what's up, Ken?" he asked.

Boom!

Ken broke into a small smile, but before he could reply, the sound of the .38 revolver echoed through the house. Wayne fell over his desk chair and tumbled to the floor, holding his chest, where a gaping hole was spewing blood.

Boom!

The gun echoed through the house once again as Kayla stood over Wayne and finished him off with a shot to the head.

Ken gathered all the paperwork as Kayla concealed the gun in her purse. He'd decided to kill Wayne rather than worrying about trying to pay him back, losing his successful restaurant in the process. It was easier to take Wayne out than it would be to remove Jarvis or the other made men of Miami.

Kayla had agreed to help him when she'd been offered a generous cut of the money. She was Ken's on-again/off-again lover. Her pretty face and big backside had fooled many; she was more gangster than the hardest niggas on the streets.

Once the dirty deed was done, the two quickly exited the house and headed back to the north side to wait for Zo's call.

CHAPTER 27

"You comin' over here or what?" Fiz asked Cutty impatiently. She'd tried three times to call him and finally had him on the line.

Cutty had just finished eating dinner and sexing Gabby in every possible position. He had no intention of getting out of bed, where he was still naked and cuddled up with his woman. "Um…somethin' came up. I'll get with you tomorrow," he said.

Gabby ran her long, red, freshly manicured nails down his chest to his semi-hard-on.

"Something came up? What the hell you mean by that? If I was giving your ass money, you'd be here. But I see how it is. You got a li'l money now, so fuck Fiz, huh?" she yelled, angry as hell that she was going to be deprived of her porn star sex that he'd promised her.

Cutty sighed and let out a light laugh. "Don't keep coming at me with the fuck shit! I told you earlier that I had something to take care of, so miss me with that bull. Like I said, I'll see you tomorrow. Now bye!" In his haste to disconnect the line, he pressed send instead of end on the phone.

Just as Fiz was about to hang up, she realized that Cutty hadn't clicked off the call, so she held the phone and listened.

Cutty laid the phone on the headboard and shook his head.

Gabby rubbed his dick, ready for another round. "Damn, baby. You musta ate that bitch's pussy or something, the way she's acting," she joked as Cutty played with her hair.

"Don't even try me. We ain't going there," he replied, moving his hands to her C-cups.

Fiz's heart skipped a beat as she listened in. She couldn't believe Cutty was fucking his cousin, or at least the girl they said was his cousin. It suddenly all made sense to her, and she could finally see why Gabby gave her attitude all the time.

"You always tryin' to get off the subject. Tell me what really happened between y'all. I promise I ain't gonna get mad," Gabby said, rubbing his balls.

"What'd I just tell you? Baby girl, we got the money, and we need to get right now, so quit trippin'. We good," Cutty said, then moved his hand down to her hairless crotch.

"A'ight, but it's over now. I ain't playin' yo' cousin no more if we straight now." Gabby leaned in and kissed him on the chest.

"Okay. That's what's up," Cutty said, pulling Gabby on top of him.

Tears began to roll down Fiz's cheeks. She couldn't believe she'd been played. The more she thought about all the money she'd given to Cutty, the madder she got. She'd crossed her real friend, her bestie, and let Cutty rob her spot, and now she was just pissed and feeling like a used fool.

"Oh yeah, baby," Gabby moaned as she slid down on

Cutty's hard dick.

"Yeah! Fuck yeah! Shit!" he moaned as she slowly started riding him.

A few minutes later, deep moans and loud cries came through the phone. Fiz's sadness and hurt suddenly turned to fury and resentment. She clicked off the line, and a plan immediately began to formulate in her head.

* * * * *

"Say, Ken, I just got with everybody, and I convinced 'em all to accept your payments and kill the beef. We gonna meet out at Tex's gambling spot, but you need to meet me at the Walmart on MLK first though. You can leave your car there and ride with me. I'm on my way now," Zo said, anxious to get rid of the Ken problem once and for all.

"A'ight. We on our way. I just gotta make one quick stop to grab the money," Ken said as Kayla navigated through Miami's backstreets.

"Don't worry about the money yet. We'll handle all that tomorrow. And who you got with you? I hope it ain't that girl, 'cause she can't go with us to the meeting," Zo said, trying to make the job easy as possible.

"She'll just drop me off," Ken said, looking over at the sexy but deadly Kayla.

"A'ight then. I'll be waiting on you," Zo answered, realizing the woman would, more than likely, have to be taken care of too. He sat back with his gun in his lap, waiting on Ken to show. A few minutes later, when he recognized the car rounding the lot, he blinked his lights.

"There he is. Go over there," Ken told Kayla.

Zo got out of his car and stood next to the unoccupied van he'd parked next to. He looked over his shoulder to make sure the coast was clear. As soon as Kayla pulled the car to a halt, Zo walked over.

"Here I come!" Ken yelled out the window as Ken made his way to their car.

"What time you want me to pick you—" Kayla asked.

Pop! Pop! Pop! Pop! Pop!

Before she could finish her question, the fire from the end of the .45 automatic lit up the end of the barrel in the pitch darkness. Zo stood at the driver-side window, squeezing the trigger. The first shit caught Kayla off guard, blowing a hole in the side of her head and sending her sideways, into Ken's lap. He then leveled the gun at his old friend.

Ken frantically tried to open the door and get out. "Hold up, man! No, Zo! What the fuck, man?" he wailed as he crouched low, praying that the shots would stop.

Zo didn't stop shooting until the clip was empty. After the last shot, the scream of a woman nearby startled him. He ran, jumped in the car, and sped out of the lot, relieved that one major problem had been taken care of—a problem that would have had Jarvis coming after him, which was a risk he wasn't willing to take.

"Ow! Oh my God, it hurts!" Ken cried out as the two shots in his shoulder and arm began to sting and burn. The vest under his clothes had stopped all the other shots from penetrating his torso. He pushed Kayla over into her seat and climbed out of the car.

Ken collapsed in the parking lot, and when he woke, he was surrounded by EMT workers and police. Later that night, heavily sedated in the hospital, there were only two things on his mind: Zo and revenge.

* * * * *

Fiz walked through Shakers, hoping Slay and Iggy, two known robbers from the west side of Atlanta, were there, looking for their next lick, like they usually were on the weekends. In the past, she'd set up robberies for the pair, but she'd quit fucking with them when they refused to pay her for one of the licks she'd hooked them up with. Most of the other dancers knew what the rough-looking men were up to; Slay and Iggy seldom ever wanted a dance or a drink, and they always lurked around the back of the club. Fiz was sure they had recruited a few of the other girls to lure the right baller into their web for a cut of the money.

As she made her way through the crowd, she spotted the thugs in their usual spot, both of them looking around suspiciously. "Hey, y'all. What's up?" she asked, taking a seat between them.

Slay looked at her sideways, while Iggy kept his attention on the crowd. "What up, Fiz?" Slay said, putting emphasis on her name.

Fiz looked at him like he smelled. "Money, nigga. What the fuck you think is up?" Fiz watched Iggy as he stared at the VIP section, where a local rapper draped in diamonds was popping bottles with his crew, showering a couple strippers with money. Fiz knew exactly what was on his mind. "Man, Iggy that there is only a li'l money. I got a lick that'll set y'all all the way right," Fiz said, seething as she thought about Cutty and Gabby fucking behind her back.

"Oh yeah?" Slay asked, looking at Fiz, with his head crooked to the side.

"Last time I set y'all niggas up with a lick, though, y'all fucked me over. Can I really trust you or not?" she asked, looking from Slay to Iggy.

"You keep bringing that old shit up. Like we told you, there weren't no money in that nigga's spot. You the one who tripped out on us," Iggy lied, knowing good and well that they'd taken two blocks and $30,000 from Cheeky after Fiz gave them the rundown on his spot.

Fiz turned her lips up, thinking back to the incident. Word on the street was that Cheeky had been found taped up, shot in the head, and robbed of a large quantity of drugs and money. "A'ight, whatever. Let's just put that shit behind us. Can we do some straight-up business this time or what?" she asked, this time looking from Iggy to Slay. "'Cause if y'all can't help me, you know I can find some other stick-up kids who can."

"Look, Fiz, we've always played fair with you, and we ain't 'bout to stop that now. So what's the move?" Slay said, leaning in to pay closer attention to her words over the loud music.

Fiz lied to the two notorious robbers who never left a soul breathing after a job. She told them, with a straight face, all about Cutty and his girl and the big money they were supposedly stashing for her uncle, who supplied all of Atlanta. "I been fuckin' this nigga behind his girl's back. One day I watched two older men in work clothes drop off a duffle bag of money and pick up two big boxes that I knew had dope in 'em. Y'all just get me $100,000, and you can have the rest."

Iggy rubbed his chin while Slay ran the numbers in his head. "Let's do this then. Just give us the info on the nigga," Iggy said, ready to roll on Cutty ASAP.

Fiz gave them the info and a whole rundown of the spot.

She also made sure they had her cell number, just in case. "So, when do y'all plan on making it happen?" she asked, eager to make Cutty pay for crossing her.

"It'll be done tonight," Slay replied as he stood and pulled his hoodie up over his head.

She smiled as she watched them leave, knowing Cutty and his bitch wouldn't live to see morning.

* * * * *

Iggy was familiar with Arbor Glen, the apartments where Cutty lived. They turned into the dark, gloomy apartment complex and looked for Apartment 114.

"Right there," Slay said, pointing at the door.

The dashboard clock read 3:32 a.m., so most of the residents in the apartment complex were asleep.

Cutty and Gabby were lying naked, spooning, knocked out after a long day of wild, crazy sex. They were sleeping so deeply that they didn't hear their would-be robbers and murderers fumbling with the front door.

When they were unsuccessful at picking the lock, Slay took a step back and sized the door up. Seconds later, the thin, wood-framed door was crashing in, and he and Iggy were running through the apartment with two pistol-grip pump-action guns in hand.

Cutty and Gabby jumped up after hearing the loud crash, but before they could get out of bed, Iggy and Slay were in their bedroom, waving the guns in their faces and demanding money and drugs.

"Give up the money and dope now!" Iggy screamed, knowing they only had a few minutes to clean house.

"Huh? What the hell you talkin' about, man? Ain't no dope or money up in here," Cutty screamed as Gabby slid behind him in the bed.

Iggy searched the room while Slay held them at gunpoint.

"Nigga, you lyin', and I'm gonna give you one minute to come clean, or both of y'all are dead," Slay said through clenched teeth.

Meanwhile, Iggy continued turning the apartment upside down. "Hmm, what we got here?" he said, pulling $45,000 out of Cutty's sock drawer. "Now where's the rest?"

"Nigga, where's the rest? Where you got the dope?" Slay screamed, knowing their time was about up.

"That's all I've got, man! Really! I do what y'all do, man. Ask anybody about Cutty! That's all of it!" he cried out.

Slay and Iggy looked at each other, then leveled their guns at the bed.

"Nigga, you lying!" Slay spat as he pulled the trigger on his pistol-grip.

Boom!

Cutty dodged the shot, moving just in time for the slug to hit Gabby, knocking her small, naked body off the bed. The slug blew a gaping hole in her chest, exposing her insides.

"No, man! No!" Cutty screamed in horror, scrambling to get away.

Boom! Boom!

He had no chance, though, because Iggy and Slay simultaneously pulled their triggers again, blowing away chunks of bloody flesh and killing him instantly. They quickly searched the apartment one more time. Knowing the police had probably already been called and would be there any minute, they finally took the $45,000 and exited the apartment, pissed. Just as they left the parking lot, a police cruiser with its blue lights blazing headed to the scene.

"That bitch lied! We searched the whole spot," Iggy said, tightly gripping the steering wheel.

"Yeah, real talk. Something ain't sittin' right wit' this shit," Slay agreed, slamming his fist into the dashboard.

CHAPTER 28

After riding all day, I was glad to be back in the city. I reluctantly called Fiz when I entered the city limits to see if she was at the apartment. I hoped she wasn't, because I really didn't feel like dealing with her fake ass while I grabbed some clothes and a few other things to hold me over while I stayed in the hotel. I huffed when I pulled up at the apartment and saw her car out front. I secured the truck, making sure the valuable cargo was well hidden, and then I climbed out.

"You back, lady!" Fiz called out from her room, as if she was really glad to see me.

I held my tongue and kept it cool, even though I really wanted to beat her ass. "Yeah, but I ain't stayin' long. I got some things to handle," I said, then hurried back to my room and started packing up what I needed. Before I was finished, she was at the door.

"Girl, what you got going on? Your ass up to something," she said playfully, as if we were all buddy-buddy or some shit.

I gave her a big, fake smile. "You know I'm on a mission

to get the money for Prime's lawyer. I refuse to just give up on him," I said, really wanting to fuck her ass up.

She looked down at my bag. "It looks like you're moving out or some shit. Where you goin', girl?" she asked in a joking tone, though I knew she was really trying to get all up in my business.

I looked at her so differently now. I hadn't been brought up to hate anyone, but at that moment, I hated Fiz with a hate beyond words. If she would have fallen over dead right in front of me, I wouldn't have given a damn. "I'm just on a money-making mission, that's all. I'll call you," I said, then walked by her and headed to the door.

"Money-makin', huh? You working tonight?" she asked, following behind me.

"Nope. I got bigger fish to fry," I said as I stepped out the door.

She stood in the doorway and watched as I pulled the truck out. I could tell she was desperate to know what I was up to, but I wasn't about to tell her.

I had decided to stay at the Red Roof Inn a few blocks from the apartment, and I called Jarvis as soon as I was settled in. "Hey, I'm in," I said, still angry that he'd forced me to pay for his help with pussy.

"Good. Where? I hope you're not at the apartment," he said like a concerned parent.

"No. The Red Roof Inn on Memorial Drive, Room 21. It's pretty quiet around here, so I'll be okay. How long can I keep the truck?" I asked, knowing it would be best to wait for nightfall to unload it.

"You don't gotta rush. I've still got the truck for a couple more days. Call me if you need me…and be careful," he said before he ended the call.

The night I'd spent with Jarvis kept playing over and over in my head. I had gone against everything I'd sworn off of when Jarvis had entered my room in his robe, but I really had no choice. Now that I had the dope, sex could no longer be used as a bargaining tool. I had only welcomed him reluctantly into my bed because I didn't want to let Prime down. From a very young age, I'd been misled about niggas, sex, and money, but now that I knew better, I wanted to do better. As Jarvis had slidden slowly in and out of me, all I could think about was Prime coming home. I felt bad when Jarvis released inside of me, then climbed out of bed.

A second later, I snapped out of my memories of the night before and began fishing through my purse, looking for the list of Prime's contacts. I made a few calls, and when some picked up, I explained the situation and told them that I was taking over for Prime until he got home. Some were reluctant to work with me, but after I laid it on thick in a boss-like way, they finally agreed. After all those phone calls, six kilos were sold.

Beep!

While I tried a couple more numbers, I heard a horn blowing out front. I peeked out the window to see who it was, and I couldn't believe who I saw. *Fiz? What the fuck?* "Bitch, how you know where to find me," I mumbled to myself as I closed the curtain back. "Damn. I knew I should have gotten a room around back. She must have spotted my truck." After all, there weren't too many big, white ESVs with rental tags riding around the city.

Beep! Beep!

She annoyingly blew the horn a couple more times, then got out the car. She walked over, looked in the truck, then got back in her car and pulled off.

I lay back on the bed and thought about my mission, waiting for the cover of darkness so I could unload my truck. Before I knew it, I'd dozed off, and I didn't wake up till two hours later, past the time when I wanted to be up. "Damn!" I cursed when I looked over at the bedside clock.

I got up, slipped my sneakers on, and grabbed the keys. I looked out the peephole to make sure the coast was clear before I opened the door. As I walked to the truck, I remembered the way Prime used to do business, and I knew I'd have to mimic him when I met with the dealers.

Just as I opened the truck door, a hand wrapped around me and covered my mouth. I was lifted up and carried back into the hotel room. I tried to catch a glimpse of my attacker in the mirror on the dresser, but I couldn't see anything before he pushed me, face first, onto the bed. I heard another man enter, and then the door closed. They duct-taped my wrists and ankles together, then pulled a pillowcase over my head and wrapped the tape around it up to my mouth so I couldn't scream. I was sure I was about to die, but instead, I heard them rummaging through the room. A few minutes later, the door opened and closed. My heart dropped when I heard the truck engine roar to life. I couldn't do anything but cry as I tried to free myself from the bonds, which took me three hours. As soon as I was free, I quickly grabbed the phone and called Jarvis.

"Hello?" he answered groggily.

I was at a loss for words, so I just broke down crying.

"Nikki? Nikki, what's wrong?" he snapped, now fully awake.

"Somebody took the truck! Oh my God, I don't know what to do! They taped me up and…oh my God! I-I don't know!" I cried.

Jarvis sat quietly on the line for a moment, then spoke. "I'm booking a flight for you. Get some rest and be at the airport in the morning. I'll text you the flight info in a minute," he said angrily, as if he doubted my story.

"Okay," I said, sobbing. I hung up and thought about what he said. I wasn't sure whether it was safe to go; for all I knew, he was ready to kill me over the loss. I lay down and closed my eyes again, but there was no use trying to sleep.

* * * * *

The next day, Zo and Jarvis sat in Jarvis's home library, going over numbers and plans for the next shipment.

"When this stuff arrives, you need to handle it. Here," he said, handing him a key to the motorcycle shop. "Make sure everything is accounted for before you accept it," Jarvis said.

"I got you," Zo said, adding the key to his own ring.

"I'll make sure they contact you an hour before they arrive with the shipment." Jarvis looked down at his vibrating cell phone. He picked it up from his lap and saw that someone was calling him from a blocked number. He ignored the call, but before he could lay the phone back down, it rang again. He ignored it again and laid it on the table. "Damn, remind me to get my number changed," he told Zo.

Ding-dong!

"Excuse me," Jarvis said, none too happy to be interrupted by the phone and now the doorbell. He stood, exited the library, and headed to the door. When he looked out the window and saw that his driver had returned from the airport, he excitedly opened the door.

* * * * *

"Hey, Nikki," he said, looking down at me from the door-way.

"Hey, Jarvis. I-I'm so, so sorry," I said sadly. I felt bad not only for Jarvis's loss but also because I had failed Prime—again. The shit was all fucked up.

He stepped to the side to let me in.

"Don't worry. We'll work it out." He leaned in and hugged me so tightly that I could feel his growing manhood up against my stomach.

"How do you work out that much money? I owe you $200,000 for that stuff," I replied.

"Come with me," he said, then led me back to his library. "Zo, this is Nikki. Nikki, this is Zo, my right-hand man," Jarvis introduced.

Zo looked me up and down like he was about to pounce on me. "What's up, Nikki?" he said, focusing on my bottom half.

"What's up?" I replied dryly.

He stood up and picked his keys up from the table. "A'ight, Jarvis, I'll holla at you later. Miss Nikki, you have a good evenin' now," he said, then walked out the big, wooden library doors. Just before the door closed behind him, he turned around. "Oh, Jarvis what you wanna do with the truck coming from Atlanta?" he asked, holding the door open.

Jarvis's eyes grew big, and he jumped up and rushed across the room toward Zo, a reaction that confused both of us. "Step outside," he ordered, then followed his man out the door.

I sat in the library, lost in thought. I was sure Fiz had to be responsible for the hotel robbery—just as responsible as she was for the one at our apartment. *I'ma have to kill this bitch if she don't quit fuckin' with Prime's money,* I thought.

* * * * *

"Just make sure all ten kilos are accounted for before you turn the truck back in," Jarvis whispered.

"A'ight. It oughtta be here in a couple hours," Zo replied, wondering why Jarvis was acting strange about the Cadillac ESV arriving from Atlanta with a small shipment.

* * * * *

A few minutes later, Jarvis returned to the finely furnished library.

"Everything cool?" I asked.

"Yeah. Now, let's get back to business, shall we? We can work out the $200,000. I'm just glad you weren't hurt. You need to stay in Miami till we can get you on your feet. That will allow us to work out this money problem too. I'm gonna set you up in my condo out on the east side and hook you up with some transportation," he said firmly, as if I had no choice.

"Jarvis, I…Prime's lawyer needs his money. I can't be lounging around in your condo while my man's depending on me to get him out," I said, meaning every word.

He looked at me as if he didn't agree. "Don't worry. I'll help you get a lawyer for him, and we'll just put it on your tab. For now, you'll be moving into the condo and driving my Porsche 911. You need to relax and take it easy, Nikki. You're way to beautiful to be worrying your pretty little head off about any of this shit. You don't even have to go back to that apartment for clothes or anything. Just take my credit card and get whatever you need." He pulled out his wallet, took out the charge card, and handed it to me.

"Thanks, Jarvis. I'm sure Fiz was behind this, too, 'cause she was the only one who knew where I was," I said, tucking the credit card in my pocket.

"Don't worry about it. I'll take care of that situation," he said firmly, then leaned in and kissed me deeply.

I tried to pull away, but he pulled me back to him. Not wanting to upset him, and thinking about Prime, I gave in and kissed him hard. I was still willing to do whatever I had to to get my man the money he needed, and for the time being, Jarvis was our only hope.

CHAPTER 29

The next night, Iggy and Slay hung around the club, waiting on Fiz to hit the floor.

After a while, she began to make her usual rounds, soliciting dances as she made her way to the back of the club. She spotted Iggy and Slay in their usual corner, and as soon as they saw her, they both stood and waved her over. She slowly made her way to where they were seated, far from the action. "What's up, y'all? I been waiting for you," she lied, picking up on their uneasiness.

"Bitch. that nigga ain't have shit up in there! You said the nigga was holding big shit, but you just sent us on a real dummy mission," Iggy barked.

Fiz was scared as hell but refused to show it. "Nigga, y'all tripping. The nigga's been stashing big dope and money. Y'all must have missed it, or else you just don't wanna give me my cut. See? I knew I shouldn't have fucked wit' y'all. I knew there was gonna to be some bullshit in the mix," Fiz said, putting on her best act.

Iggy and Slay refused to buy it.

"Bitch, you must think we're stupid. We put this shit together, and now you owe us for killing that nigga and his bitch. We don't know which one you had beef with, but it's $75,000 a head, and we're gonna need that $150,000 by next week. Bitch, you better never try us like that again," Slay said in a sinister tone.

Fiz was so caught up in Slay's demands and threats and the fact that he was getting all up in her face that she didn't see Iggy when he brought down an eight-inch blade and sliced her from her forehead all the down the side of her face to her to her chin. The gash opened her face like a piece of ripe fruit. "Ah!" she screamed, grabbing the wound.

Iggy then jammed the knife in her leg.

"Ow!" she screamed, but her cries were muffled by the loud music blasting from the sound system. She bent down and grabbed her leg where the knife had punctured her and chipped her bone. Blood was flowing from both wounds as she fell to the floor.

"Bitch, get that hundred and fifty grand," Slay said, bending down to position his mouth next to her ear.

Iggy grabbed a handful of her hair and used it to clean her blood off the knife before they disappeared into the crowd.

Fiz lay there helplessly, dazed, hurting and confused, while her blood soaked into the carpet. One of the other dancers finally noticed her and called for help. Thirty minutes later, Fiz's face and leg was being treated by local paramedics while two Atlanta policemen questioned her about her injuries that would most definitely put her out of work for a while. She didn't hesitate to give the officers a detailed description of Slay and Iggy.

After the EMTs treated her, she ran her hand down the large

bandage that was positioned over the cut running down the side of her face; it had required close to twenty stitches. Knowing she would never be able to come up with the $150,000 they had demanded, she informed the police about a possible double-homicide the two might have been responsible for.

The officers took her statement and went through one more round of questions before they packed up and left, leaving their business cards with her. "If you think of anything else, give us a call," the taller of the two said.

"Girl, you gonna be straight again soon," said Coco, the dancer who'd called for help. "Yeah thanks," Fiz said, limping over to her BMW. She was scared and mad, and on the way to her apartment, she picked up the phone and called Jarvis.

"Hello?" he answered dryly, not to happy to see her number.

"Hey, baby. Shit been crazy around here. How have you been?" she said slowly, trying not to aggravate her face wound.

Jarvis frowned hard. "Why you callin' me now, you scandalous, lying bitch? Lose my damn number! I don't ever want to hear your voice again," he snapped as he lay in bed.

"Jarvis, hold up. What's going on? What are you talking about?" Fiz screamed, weaving in and out of the late-night traffic.

"You fuckin' disappear and go screwin' around with a bunch of niggas like a gold-digging ho, and now you just come back around, hopin' I'll be so glad to hear from you that I'll empty my wallet? You out fucking big ballers for money? Bitch, you got me fucked up! You're dead to me. Have a nice life, and if you don't stay out of mine, I'll cancel you just like I did that credit card I gave you," he spat, then hung up the phone.

"No that bitch didn't!" Fiz screamed, slapping the steering wheel and causing the car to swerve.

* * * * *

I lay in the king-sized bed in Jarvis's half-million-dollar condo, tossing and turning. I couldn't get Prime off my mind. He probably called the apartment looking for me, and I hoped he didn't think I'd turned my back on him. I was in deep debt with Jarvis, and after he paid for Prime's lawyer, I'd be in even deeper, but I didn't care. The important thing was that Prime got what he needed to be free.

Jarvis had called an hour earlier to let me know that he couldn't sleep and would be stopping by. I looked at the clock and saw that it was 2:00 a.m., so I knew what was on his mind. Despite my earlier promises to myself, I had to go along with whatever Jarvis wanted, at least until Prime had enough money for the high-priced attorney who could help him win his court case.

My ringing cell phone jarred me from my thoughts, and I saw Fiz's number on the caller ID. "Hello?" I answered, assuming she was just leaving the club.

"You backstabbing-ass ho! How in the hell could you go and tell Jarvis all that shit? I trusted your mutt ass, but don't even trip now. When I run across yo' ass, get ready for the beating yo' mama shoulda gave you a long time ago! Ho, you're mine!" she threatened, screaming at the top of her lungs.

I couldn't believe Jarvis had told her what I'd said, but after thinking about it, I really didn't give a fuck about her or her threats. "Fuck-ass ho! Hell yeah I told him. I know you were behind those robberies, so you deserve whatever comes to your trifling ass! You say I'm yours, huh? Nah, bitch, you're mine!" I snapped, raising up in the bed.

"Okay then, bitch. We'll see. I'm on my way to your hotel

room right now, and I'll show your ass a thing or two," she yelled as she exceeded the speed limit while digging in the glove box for her can of mace.

I laughed. "Hotel? You stupid slut. I'm in Miami, sleeping in Jarvis's nice-ass condo, with a candy apple-red convertible Porsche sitting outside. I'll be driving that shit while I spend his money. Your ex-man is taking good care of me now, ho, so sweet dreams, Fizzy, boo," I said, toying with her name just to antagonize her.

After I hung up, I tossed my phone to the side, climbed back under the comforters, and dozed off.

Jarvis awakened me when he entered the condo in the middle of the night. Minutes later, he was naked, climbing in bed. "Mmm…yeah," he moaned as he slid his short, fat, hard erection inside of me.

"Oh!" I called out as he dug deep, giving me all of him, which wasn't much. I tried my best to picture Prime on top of me while he gave me a feeling that I only thought Prime could give.

"Oh, Nikki, baby," he cried out as he sexed me slow and steady.

I tried my best to hold my cries of pleasure in, but it just felt too good. "Ah, Jarvis, yes! God, yes!" I screamed out in pleasure, feeling bad and ashamed.

Jarvis didn't fuck me; instead, he made slow, passionate love to me until we both collapsed in one another's arms.

When I woke the next morning, he was gone.

CHAPTER 30

One week later...

"So...what, exactly, are you telling me?" Prime asked Dan Senegal, one of the nation's most successful defense attorneys.

"I'm telling you that if they take this to trial, we're going to have them for breakfast, lunch, and dinner. This is a clear-cut case of entrapment, not to mention illegal search and seizure. It will take a while for us to get all your possessions back though," he said as he pulled off his gold-framed Ralph Lauren glasses and pinched the bridge of his nose.

"I ain't worried about property or any of that stuff. I'm just ready to be outta here," Prime stressed as he sat across from Dan in the small, cold, glass-enclosed room reserved for attorney visits.

Dan placed his glasses back on his long, pointed nose and shuffled through some papers until he found what he was looking for. "Who is this guy?" he asked Prime, holding up a photo of Big.

"An old friend," Prime said sarcastically, looking angrily at the mugshot.

"With friends like him, who needs enemies? He's all they've got right now, but I've checked him out pretty thoroughly, and it looks like we can put in an order to have his testimony suppressed. If we can keep him off the stand, it'll be the fatal dagger in the prosecutor's case. Right now, we are looking good, so get ready to walk in that courtroom Monday and tear them a new asshole," Dan said. He stuffed the documents back in his briefcase and clicked the gold latch locks until they engaged.

Prime smiled from ear to ear. From the first moment he'd met Dan, he'd recognized that he was one of the best in the business. The man had a definite energy and intelligence about him, and the hefty price tag for his services spoke volumes. Prime had also heard all the stories about Dan being a beast in the courtroom, the Johnnie Cochran of Atlanta. "I'm past ready," Prime said, feeling good about how things were playing out.

Dan got up, grabbed his visitor's badge, and clipped it on his shirt pocket. See you Monday," he said, stepping out the door and into the hall, where a guard was waiting to escort him back down to the lobby.

On the way back to his cell, Prime was permitted one call. When no one answered at the apartment, he left a message that he'd be going to court Monday.

When Fiz checked the messages later that evening, she smiled, thinking of her next move.

* * * * *

I had been in close contact with Dan, and outside of his

high fee, he was a good man. He had called Jarvis and me to let us know that Prime's court date was set for Monday, and he assured me that Prime had an excellent chance of walking out a free man. I couldn't wait. I hadn't seen him since he'd left the house on the day of his arrest, and I'd only talked to him once since then.

Jarvis and I had a flight booked from Miami to Atlanta Sunday evening. Since I'd been staying in Jarvis's condo, things had gotten real personal between us. Honestly, his generosity and late-night lovemaking had my feeling kind of tied up. I had to fight myself daily not to fall for the shallow life Jarvis was trying to push on me. In Miami, I'd been well taken care of in every way, and I'd wanted for nothing. I played the part of Jarvis's love interest while waiting for Prime to come home. I was sure Jarvis thought he could win me over, but my love for Prime outweighed anything he could give me mentally, sexually, and spiritually. I had been stashing the money he'd been giving me so Prime would have money to do whatever he needed when he came home.

I was nervous and excited for Monday to come. Fiz had been blowing up mine and Jarvis's phones, calling from a private number. The calls didn't stop until we both had our numbers changed.

"So Prime's court date is Monday, huh?" Jarvis asked as we sat in the TV room watching a movie, scarfing down pizza.

"Yeah. You already know, Jarvis. We got plane tickets and everything," I replied, knowing he was just being smart.

"You happy about it?" he asked, wiping his hands on a napkin and looking at me.

I looked into his eyes. "Yeah. I pray he beats this shit," I said with more excitement than I meant to show. I missed Prime like crazy, and I could tell Jarvis wasn't too pleased about that.

"So what happens to us when he comes back?" Jarvis asked, sliding over close to me.

I didn't have an answer. As of late, I'd really been enjoying Jarvis's company, but Prime coming home was another thing. I paused as I thought about his question; I truly didn't know how to answer. "What do you mean?" I asked, trying to run my words through my head, making sure they came out right.

He looked at me with a serious expression on his face. "It's a simple question, Nikki. What happens to us when he comes home?" he asked again, this time with a hint of anger in his tone.

I looked at him with puppy eyes. "Just being honest, Jarvis, I don't know. I think about it all the time, especially since we've gotten closer. Can we just let things play out as they will and deal with them as they come? I just...I really don't know," I said, feeling like I was betraying Prime.

At that time in my life, I realized that I had no control over my feelings. As much as I tried to keep them bottled up, they kept coming out—and not just for Prime but for Jarvis as well. I had never meant for things to go so far with Jarvis, but it was out of my control. The one thing I did know was that I'd always be Jarvis's friend, because he had come through for me in a big way when I most needed a helping hand.

"Just know that I love and care for you unconditionally, Nikki. Never forget that," he said, then leaned in and kissed me.

I felt as if I'd known Jarvis for years, and we connected in a way I'd never expected. "I won't," I mumbled through our kisses.

Before long, he had my skirt pulled up and his head buried between my legs. He sucked and licked my clit until I trembled. He then pulled his pants down and entered my wetness.

CHAPTER 31

Iggy and Slay were chilling out at the local gameroom when two police cars whipped into the lot. Following behind them were three unmarked official cars. Slay was caught off guard when the police and detectives jumped out and rushed inside.

The three dealers who were off in the back playing pool quickly tossed their sacks of crack and weed into the pockets of the pool table.

Iggy was back in the bathroom when they stormed the establishment. He and Slay had no idea they were on the State's most wanted list for the double-murder they'd recently committed, but the police had been on their trail since finding out their true identities.

"Get down now!" the police screamed as they pointed their gun at all the men in the room.

Iggy had just wiped his ass and was getting up when he heard all the commotion out front. He cracked the bathroom door and saw several officers making their way through the building. He didn't know if they were looking for him or just raiding the place, but he wasn't about to stick around to find out. He rushed over to the window, eased it up, and climbed out. Just as he dropped outside, more police were rounding the building.

"Freeze!" two uniformed officers screamed in unison, leveling their guns at him.

Iggy ignored them and took off through the woods. Without looking back, he ran at full speed, dodging the hanging branches and tree limbs. Just as he thought he was in the clear, he tumbled over a big rock and fell, face first, in the high brush.

The officer on his heels dived on top of him and pinned him to the ground, where he held him until his partner reached the scene. "Gotcha, asshole!" he said as he cuffed Iggy and escorted him back to the car, where a handcuffed Slay already sat. "Get in," the officer said, then shoved Iggy inside.

Iggy and Slay looked at each other and just shook their heads in disgust.

"What the fuck is this all about? What we charged with?" Iggy screamed from the back seat as Slay dropped his head.

"Aggravated assault and double-homicide," the officer replied, all calm and cool, as he buckled up. "You young punks will never learn. Why the fuck would you cut a young lady up in public when she already knows all about your dirty deeds?" The officer laughed at them in his rearview mirror, then put the car and drive and pulled out of the lot.

Iggy didn't reply, but he now knew the source of their misery, the one who'd ratted them out. "I'ma get that bitch, my nigga," he whispered to Slay.

Slay was sure they wouldn't get the chance to get even, but he nodded in silent agreement and continued to hang his head.

CHAPTER 32

We sat in the back of the courtroom, anxiously waiting for the trial to start. Prime had talked to Dan before the trial, and the lawyer had all but guaranteed him a not-guilty verdict.

My eyes lit up when Prime entered the room from a side door. He looked fine as hell in the cream-colored linen suit I'd chosen for him to wear during trial. He looked at me as I sat next to Jarvis on the front row; he grinned with a smile Jarvis envied but had to respect. He'd even gained a few muscles in prison. He scanned the room, then took a seat behind the defendant's table.

"All rise!" the bailiff called out as the black, middle-aged, stern-looking judge entered and took her position on the bench.

Everyone stood until the judge was seated. Dan and the prosecutor took the floor and started presenting their cases. An hour later, Dan had the prosecutor looking like a bumbling fool. He threw everything but the kitchen sink at the Feds' case.

Prime and I continued making eye contact throughout the

trial. I damn near melted every time he looked over at me and smiled. I could tell Jarvis was getting aggravated by our public display of affection, but just seeing Prime again had me looking at Jarvis differently. I felt bad for even sharing my heart with Jarvis, something that had totally been out of my control. I was an emotional messed, feeling crazy and all fucked up, like my heart was caught in a game of tug-o-war.

The whole courtroom fell silent as Big was escorted in to testify.

If looks could have killed, Big would have fallen dead right there from the stare Prime was giving him. He refused to make eye contact with Prime as he took the stand.

"Mr. Darious Day, could you please let the court know who your direct connect in the drug trade was? If that person is in this courtroom, please point the individual out so we will all be on the same page when I let the court know just how much dirty money and drugs the man in question was moving through the States for his illegal enterprise, an enterprise that is growing by the day," the prosecutor exaggerated, scowling at Prime.

Big looked around the courtroom and set his gaze on Prime. Big knew he'd already broken one of the major laws of the streets by working with the police, but putting his disloyalty on display in a room full of people was going overboard for him.

The prosecutor walked over in front of him while he sat on the witness stand. "Point at your connect for us, Mr. Day," the prosecutor said again.

Big looked around and shook his head from side to side. "Can't. He ain't here," he mumbled.

"Excuse me? Sir, could you please speak up for the court?" the judge asked, looking over her glasses at him.

The prosecutor thought he'd heard wrong until he heard it

again.

"He's not in here," Big said again, louder this time.

The prosecutor snatched his glasses off and stomped over to his table, knowing Big had just crushed his last hope of some kind of guilty verdict. The whole courtroom went quiet, and then a lot of loud chattering started.

"Order! Quiet in the court!" the judge called out, slamming her gavel down.

Dan walked to the middle of the floor and addressed the judge as Big left the stand. "Your Honor, we request an acquittal, in light of these events, as well as a not-guilty verdict. The prosecutor has not proven his case against my client. This is a classic case of entrapment, and the State's main witness is not able to point out the defendant as a guilty party. This whole proceeding has been a big waste of the State's time and money, and there are no grounds on which to charge my client. Thus, we respectfully ask the court to dismiss all charges and release my client without prejudice." Dan knew the judge was bound by law, no matter what Prime had been caught doing, and Big's refusal to testify required her to let Prime go.

The judge rolled her eyes at the prosecutor, who couldn't even give a rebuttal. "Case dismissed. Bailiff, please release the defendant from custody," the judge announced.

Prime smiled from ear to ear. He stood up, turned around, and blew me a kiss. Jarvis gave me a fake smile as they led Prime back to the back to be processed out.

Meanwhile, Fiz was watching all the action from the back of the room behind big shades and a wig, and she left as soon as the judge dismissed the case.

* * * * *

"Man I appreciate you. My word, I'm gonna take care of what we owe you," Prime told Jarvis as we cruised down Peachtree Street, headed to Ruth's Chris for dinner before we headed in.

"No problem. I'm pretty sure we'll be able to work something out. Being that the Feds confiscated your property, where are you looking to reside?" Jarvis asked, more interested in where I'd be than Prime having somewhere to stay.

"I spoke with Dan about all that, and he told me it'll be a lengthy process to get my shit back. I got some family on the west side. I'll reach out to them, so we'll be straight. I just need to get my feet back in the sand," Prime replied as we turned into the lot.

"That can be arranged," Jarvis said, pulling up in front of the restaurant.

"Yeah, we need to discuss that," Prime added.

"We will. Y'all have a good dinner. I know you've got a lot to talk about. I'm going to turn a block or two. Just call when you're ready," Jarvis said, looking up at me through the rearview mirror.

I looked up and caught his eye as I opened the back door of the Lincoln to get out.

"Thanks again, man I got you," Prime told him again as he got out.

I turned around before we entered and saw Jarvis just staring at us. I felt bad as he pulled away from the curb.

"Baby, you know I appreciate you holding me down, making sure I got a good lawyer and all. I been missing you like crazy too," he said, leaning in to kiss my ear.

"You know I'm down for my boo. I got ya back," I replied, so glad to be in my true love's arms again.

The waiter gave us two menus and showed us to our table. "I'll be back shortly to take your order," he said before he walked off.

I couldn't stop smiling as I gazed across the table at Prime; I knew he was going to give me the business on a whole other level later.

"So, baby, how'd you get Jarvis to give us the money for the lawyer? Fiz musta got in his ear," he said, proud of my accomplishments.

I really didn't know where to start, because ever since the day Prime had been arrested, my life had been a rollercoaster ride. He didn't know the half of it. I thought about lying to him but thought better of it; one day he would find out the truth anyway, and I figured he should hear it from me. "Baby, it's a long story," I said, hoping I could put it off.

"So?" he said, prompting me to go on.

"Okay. Let's see. Where should I start? Uh…I started working with Fiz and—"

He cut me off right there. "At Shakers?" He frowned. "Stripping and dancing?"

I looked at him and smirked, hoping he wouldn't start tripping. "Baby, don't make this hard for me now," I said, pouting.

"Go ahead," he said with a hint of anger in his tone.

"Well, I started working at Shakers 'cause I was willing to do what had to be done to get you a lawyer. I refused to let you down. I raised $93,000, but Fiz sent a nigga up in the apartment to rob me, so I was back to zero," I explained, thinking back on the night of the robbery.

"What!? Fiz set you up?" he asked, surprised.

"Yeah. I put two and two together and figured out that conniving bitch had set it all up, so I asked Jarvis for help. He was pissed about Fiz and agreed to help me out, so I hit your friends up to see if they wanted to shop, but before I could get to them, I was robbed again at the hotel for the ten kilos he'd fronted me," I explained.

The look on Prime's face made it clear that he didn't like what I was telling him. "How much?" he asked, looking at me like I was crazy.

I dropped my head. "Ten kilos," I repeated.

"You got taken for ten bricks? What the hell did Jarvis say about that?" Prime asked, trying to figure out why, after I lost the dope, he was still looking out for me.

"He told me not to trip it and promised that he'd look into it. I still owe him $200,000 for it though," I said, sounding naïve.

"So where you been staying if you ain't be fucking with Fiz?" he asked curiously, looking at me like he was about to blow.

"That's another thing. I've been staying in Miami in one of his properties, driving one of his cars. It was just until you got out."

Prime looked like he wanted to snatch me across the table. He leaned back in his seat and took a deep breath. "Lemme get this straight. Fiz set you up to be robbed. Jarvis fronted you a play, and you got robbed again, but he told you not to trip over ten bricks. He moved you to Miami and gave you a car to drive. So what happened to him and Fiz?" he asked, trying to figure it all out.

"He's not fucking with her no more after all that shady shit she pulled," I said, knowing what he was getting at.

"You telling me this nigga gave you ten bricks, a place to

stay, a car, and over 100 grand for a lawyer just like that? What are you giving him, Nikki?" he asked accusingly as the waiter came back to take our order.

I was stuck like a deer in headlights.

The waiter stood at the table and gave me a few seconds to think. "What will you lovely people be having tonight?" he asked, positioning his pen to take our order.

"We're not ready," Prime snapped, shooing the waiter away. "I asked you what you're giving him?" he asked again through clenched teeth.

"I ain't give him shit!" I blurted out, lying and trying my best to hide my guilt.

Prime leaned in close, almost in my face. "Nikki, you're fuckin' lying to me," he said, looking into my eyes.

I tried my best to keep my composure but couldn't hold it in any longer and broke down crying. "Why are you doing me like this? I did whatever I had to do to get you home! You don't know the shit I've been through for you. It doesn't matter if I fucked him or not, long as you got that money you needed. I fuckin' love you, nigga. Can't you see that?" I cried out, drawing looks from the other diners.

Prime sat back in his chair again, gave me a fucked-up look, and then just stared at me. Five minutes passed before he spoke again. "It's all good. I-I ain't mad at you," he said in an insincere way.

When the waiter came back, we ordered, then had a quiet dinner and called for the check.

When we were finished, I pulled out my cell and called Jarvis to let him know we were ready to go.

Prime looked like he wanted to slap me silly when I pulled out Jarvis's credit card to pay for the dinner. For once, I wished

I'd have brought cash. "So you got this nigga's card too?" he hissed as he walked out.

We stood out front without a word spoken between us as we waited for Jarvis to show. A few minutes later, he turned into the lot. The ride back was awkward; Prime was not his usual self after I filled him in on the details. He and Jarvis made small talk while I sat in the back, wiping away silent tears.

We eventually pulled up at the French Quarters, where I had two rooms reserved. After getting our room keys, we got on the elevator.

Prime started asking Jarvis questions, trying to pick his brains. Before we got off the elevator, Prime stepped to Jarvis who knew something was in the air. "I'm going to get you the money back for the lawyer and the $200,000 for the play she was responsible for, but I need you to give me a jumpstart. I can have your money back in a month's time," Prime said as we exited the elevator and started to our room.

I kept quiet as I walked beside Prime, listening in.

Jarvis looked at Prime and stopped in the middle if the hall. "How about we talk business in my room, just me and you? It's not that I have a problem with Nikki being present, but I think we need to have a man-to-man talk since we're about to be partners," Jarvis said, looking down at the keycard then up at the number on the door.

I glanced around Prime at Jarvis and gave him a look, praying he'd spare Prime the details about the two of us and how close we'd gotten. "That's cool. I'm beat anyway," I said then continued on to my room. I looked down the hall before going into my room and watched as Prime followed Jarvis into his suite.

* * * * *

"So you fucking my lady, huh?" Prime asked Jarvis, drawing a blank stare from the man as they both took a seat at the table.

"What makes you think that?" Jarvis asked, clasping his hands in front of him and interlocking his fingers.

Prime looked at him with a firm look on his face. "Man, I ain't slow or blind. I see what's up. You don't just write off $200,000, put somebody up in a spot, give them a car, and spend another grip on a lawyer just on the strength. What's going on, straight up?" Prime asked, then crossed his arms across his chest.

Jarvis returned his gaze for a minute before he said, "I'm gonna give you $5,000 cash, five kilos, and kill your tab. All I want you to do is disappear," Jarvis said, hoping Prime would accept his offer. He desperately wanted Prime out of the picture, no matter the cost. He hoped he would take the money and run so things wouldn't have to go to the extreme.

"What you saying?" Prime asked, balling his face up.

"You heard me. All of that is your if you get out of Nikki's life," Jarvis said, studying Prime's hard expression.

Prime let out a light laugh. "You diggin' her that much, huh? She means that much to you? It's like that?" Prime was dumbfounded that Nikki had hooked up with someone else, but he tried to hide his hurt and anger.

Jarvis nodded his head slowly. "We've been spending a lot of nights together, and I've honestly grown very fond of her. Young brother, I'm afraid you don't know your woman like you think you do. She wants things you can't provide. Just bein' real, I'll always be around. Man to man, I've been fucking Nikki since you've been gone. She came to me for help, and shit just happened. I advise you to just take my offer and get back on your feet," Jarvis said, not a bit afraid of the hard scowl on Prime's face.

"So it's that deep with y'all?" Prime wanted to snap, but he knew it wasn't Jarvis's fault that shit had gone down the way it had.

Jarvis watched Prime squirm around in his seat like his nerves were getting the best if him. "Yeah, real deep. Here's all the cash I have on hand at the moment. I'll have the five kilos delivered to you tomorrow evening, and the remainder of the $5,000 will be with the delivery."

Prime looked at the money Jarvis had set on the table in front of him and thought about it all for a minute. "I see you're dead serious," he said, tapping his fingers on the table to think about it all.

Jarvis got real serious. "I'm a businessman, Prime. I don't say what I don't mean. Now be smart and make shit happen for yourself. If you don't accept my offer, being with Nikki will only complicate your life," Jarvis said, making sure Prime picked up on his idle threat.

Prime looked across the table at Jarvis. "Complicate it, huh? Shit, my whole life's been filled with complications, and I've taken care of 'em all. I live for that shit," Prime replied, letting him know he wasn't scared. "Have the dope delivered with the rest of the money by noon tomorrow, and I'll disappear on my own terms. I'll be gone within twenty-four hours," Prime said, looking for a pen and scrap of paper.

"Deal." Jarvis extended his hand to Prime, who grabbed it in a tight grip.

"The address," Prime said, handing Jarvis the scrap of paper.

Jarvis took the paper and looked at it. "Good doing business with you…and take it easy on Nikki tonight, bruh. I know it's been a while," he added, trying to sound playful, but he really hated the night's living arrangements.

"No need to worry. I've got no desire for that. She's been in your bed all this time, and that's where she needs to stay," Prime said, tucking the money in his pocket and walking to the door.

* * * * *

Knock! Knock!

I didn't know what to expect from Prime after he and Jarvis had their little talk, but I crossed my fingers and opened the door.

Prime stepped in, looking me up and down.

"Everything all right?" I asked, closing the door behind him. I had been around Prime for the longest, and I could tell by the look on his face that something was bothering him.

"Yeah, shit straight," he said dryly. He crossed the room, pulled a stack of money from his pocket, and laid it on the table.

I walked over, looked down at the cash, then up at him. "Where'd you get that from?" I asked curiously.

Smack!

Just as I asked the question, a hard slap caught me by surprise.

"Ah!" I cried out as the force of the slap knocked me to my knees.

"So you been fucking that nigga on the regular, huh, bitch? That's some real bullshit after all I did for your punk ass! I ain't been gone but a minute, and you already fucking another nigga! You might as well go on down to that nigga's room," he screamed, standing over me with his fist balled up.

I curled up on the floor, and my chest began to hurt. I couldn't believe he was putting me through that after all I'd done to help him get the money for his lawyer. "Prime, baby, please stop! I did all I did to help you. If I wouldn't have slept with him, you'd still be sitting down in that hell hole. I only did it to get you home." I wiped the tears from my face, looking up at him.

He just looked at me without saying a word because he knew it was true. "He just offered me $5,000 and five bricks to leave you," he said, walking over to the table.

I sat up on the bed, tripping on what he'd just said. "What!?"

Prime walked back over to the bed. "He offered me five grand and five bricks to leave you. Oh, and on top of that, all the debt will be cleared," he repeated, looking at me like he hated me.

"He's gotta be tripping! What did you tell him?" I asked. The question was out of my mouth before I put two and two together. I dropped my head as I thought about the money Prime had set on the table.

He turned, grabbed the money off the table, and exited the room without looking back.

I started to open my mouth to beg him to stay, but no words would come out. The best day of my life had turned into the worst, just as bad as the day my parents were killed. "God, no," I whispered as I climbed up on the bed and cried.

Tap-tap.

A light knock on the door got my attention. I got up, walked over, and opened the door. Prime and Jarvis were standing there, naked. They both walked in and led me over to the bed.

NIKKI

They took turns fucking me until I couldn't take it anymore. Jarvis pounded me from the back while Prime fucked me in the mouth. Out of nowhere, both of them just started laughing. I started laughing, too, up until my mom and dad walked in, also naked.

Suddenly I jumped up, shaking and sweating, realizing it had all been a sick nightmare. I tried my best to fall back to sleep, but I was too afraid of dreaming again.

CHAPTER 33

Two weeks later...

Ken sat outside of Zo's townhouse in a tinted-out Toyota Avalon, waiting for him to come out. After his brief hospital stay, he'd vowed to make Zo suffer for his actions. The streetlights were shining brightly, and everything was quiet in the parking lot of the upscale community. Ken had seen Zo enter his spot earlier and had been waiting on him to come out; he didn't care if he had to wait for days, and he refused to leave till he had handled his business. The later it got, though, the harder it was for him not to just walk up, knock on the door, and blow Zo's face off when he answered. He pulled a candy bar out of the brown paper bag that he had just bought from the corner store and bit into it.

Just as he picked up his soda and took a swig, a figure moved in the darkness.

"Nigga, don't fuckin' move," Zo said with venom in his voice, pressing his Glock against the side of Ken's head.

Ken almost pissed his pants. He couldn't believe he'd gotten caught slipping. "Whoa, man!" he called out, holding his hands in the air like he was under arrest.

Zo recognized the voice instantly. He snatched the hat off Ken's head to make sure his mind wasn't playing tricks on him. Zo had spotted the car following him earlier and had waited on darkness so he could move in while it sat outside of his townhouse. He knew the man wasn't undercover or police because he moved too sloppily and stuck out like a sore thumb in the bright blue ride. "Ni-nigga, you ain't dead?" Zo snatched the car door open and jerked Ken out by his jacket collar.

Ken didn't resist as Zo kept the Glock pressed to the side of his head. "Zo, man, I just came to holla at you, man. Don't do it like this, li'l bro. Shit, I'm the one who gave you the game, right?" Ken knew he had to get to the .38 he had tucked in the small of his back, and he had to do it fast.

"Nah, nigga, it's over. This time I'm gonna make sure you ain't breathing no mo'," Zo said as he dragged him down the hill next to the creek than ran behind the townhomes. When Zo got him to the heavily wooded area, he slammed the Glock into the back of Ken's head, knocking him to his knees. "I gave you a chance to get outta Dodge, and your stubborn ass had to stay. It's over now, nigga," Zo said.

Click!

Zo placed the barrel to the back of his head and pulled the trigger.

Ken squeezed his eyes shut, anticipating a gun blast that never came. He opened his eyes and realized that Zo's gun had jammed. He fumbled for his .38, and by the time Zo was clearing the chamber on the Glock, Ken was coming up with the revolver.

Boom! Boom!

Ken pulled the trigger twice, and the barrel lit up in the darkness. The first shot struck Zo in the stomach, doubling him over, and the second pierced the top of his head. Zo fell into the thick brush, lifeless. Ken walked over and pushed him down the hill into the creek, then wiped the sweat from his forehead, thanking God that he'd somehow cheated death twice. Now all he wanted to do was to get his face right in the street.

He walked back through the darkness to his car. Before he pulled away, he pulled a small plastic bag out of his pocket, dipped his finger in it, and sniffed all the white powder off, then licked the remaining residue from his finger.

* * * * *

As Ken drove through Miami, he made several calls. His second was to Jarvis.

"Hello?" Jarvis answered, not recognizing the number on his caller ID.

"Hey, old buddy. I need to holla at ya," Ken said, making his way down Twenty-Third Avenue.

Jarvis couldn't believe his ears; Zo had given his word that Ken had been taken care of. "Who the fuck is this?" he asked.

"It's me, Ken, man. I got yo' number out of Zo's phone. I'm still alive and breathin', and I want to make things right. I know lotsa niggas are out to get me, but I ain't 'bout to let it go down like that. I'm ready to pay what I owe and clean my face," Ken said, pulling up in front of his spot.

Jarvis couldn't believe it. He was furious because, on Zo's word, he'd already told the other bosses that Ken had been taken care of. They knew he was close with Ken, and now they would think that Jarvis was lying just to protect him.

Fortunately, Jarvis knew just how to handle the mess Zo's lie had made. "I think we can work things out, as long as you got the money to satisfy everybody," Jarvis said, grabbing his cell phone and dialing Zo's number.

Ken could tell that Jarvis was doing something on the other end. He listened closely, and when he heard Zo's voicemail in the background, he smiled. "I appreciate ya, fam'. By the way, I'm afraid I had to handle ya boy Zo. Just know he wasn't good for your team. He disobeyed orders and let me live, so I rewarded him for it," Ken said, getting out of the car.

Jarvis didn't know what to think, but since Ken was ready to pay, he couldn't turn him away. After the debt was settled, it would be a different story. *Once a target, always a target,* he thought. It was a rule Ken should have known well, considering that he played by the same rule. "I'll get with the fam'. We've got our annual get-together on *Jezebel* tomorrow, so I'll set it up for then," Jarvis said.

"That boy Willie still doin' his thang? Damn, I been outta touch," Ken said, recalling the yacht where the city's heavy hitters gathered once a year.

"You know Willie. He thinks he's Puffy or some shit. I'll call and let everybody know you're coming to clear your name. Just make sure you take care of everybody…and a li'l extra would be a good gesture," Jarvis said, still pissed that Zo had lied to him—a lie that could have put the whole crew in the midst of retribution from a marked man.

"Yeah, I'll take care of everybody and maybe throw in a few tips," Ken said, thrilled for the chance to make amends and join the ranks of his old crew again.

"Tomorrow at 2:00 then," Jarvis said, then hung up. In way, he regretted that Zo was gone, but in another way, he was glad; it infuriated him to be lied to and betrayed. He ran his hand over his face, dreading having to tell the other bosses the truth.

* * * * *

The next day, I called Prime at least ten times, but he still wouldn't answer my calls. I had been calling him daily for the last two weeks, ever since he'd stormed out of the hotel room, but all I ever got was his voicemail. After he left, he gave me no choice but to go back to Miami with Jarvis. I thought about confronting Jarvis about the proposal he'd offered Prime, but I decided it was best to just let it go, considering that whatever it was, Prime had just accepted it and left, like I didn't mean shit to him. I couldn't believe he could do that, especially after I'd stooped so low, selling my most precious possession just to get the money he needed. My tears were long gone, and I hated the way I felt about Prime. I felt bad for hoping he'd get locked up again, but the way he'd fucked me over without ever hearing me out made it hard to care much about him. The first two days after he left had been hard, but I'd finally gotten comfortable in my new life with Jarvis. Still, every time I said, "Fuck Prime!" I found myself calling him again.

"I'm out. I'll call you later." Jarvis kissed me softly on the lips before heading out to his annual get-together on his friend Willie's yacht.

As soon as he was out the door, I called Prime. "Fuck you, Prime!" I screamed in his voicemail as my eyes watered.

* * * * *

Ken walked across the lot carrying a big canvas bag.

At the walkway of the yacht, Jarvis and the other bosses

were huddled together, staring at him suspiciously and whispering.

"Yo, family, what's up?" Ken asked nervously as he entered the circle of men he'd borrowed money from but had never repaid.

"What up, nigga? You got my money?" asked Freeze, one of Miami's deadliest bosses.

Ken knew he was walking on thin ice with the whole crew, as he'd played them and had majorly disrespected them. The same men who'd once looked at him like family now shunned him, and he couldn't really blame them. "I got all y'all's money…and I gotta apologize for my actions. Shit was just crazy in my life, man. I know that ain't no excuse, but it's the truth. It's a long story that I don't wanna bore y'all with, but I'm here today to settle my tab and make everything right. Y'all are my brothers. Please forgive me for my transgressions and let me make amends," he said, pouring out his heart to the other bosses.

Styles, the true businessman of the crew, stuck his hands in the pockets of his cargo shorts and frowned. "Maybe we can do that, as long as you've got everybody's money. And from now on, you're gon' have to pay a fee every month to operate in this city. We been talking this over, and we think it's only fair. Straight up, you don't even deserve to be living," he said, and the others nodded in agreement.

"A fee? C'mon, y'all!" Ken walked behind the men as they boarded *Jezebel* to enjoy the late lunch the chef had laid out in the lower level for them.

"No ifs, ands, or buts about it, it's gonna be $6,000 a month to operate. We'll all split that between us. I think it's a bargain for all the troubles you've put us through," Styles said.

Ken knew he was lucky to still be breathing, and he wanted

NIKKI

to get rid of the bad blood between them, so he had no choice but to agree to their terms. "Okay, fine. I just hope we can look into doing away with this fee down the line," he said.

All the men took their seat around the large glass table.

"That might happen in due time, once you prove yourself worthy of our trust again," Jarvis added.

As the men ate turkey and pastrami sandwiches and laughed about old times, the yacht pulled out of the bay and entered the Atlantic.

"Man, you remember when you used to drive around the city in that old Cadillac Seville like you was some kind of pimp or some shit?" Lucci, the only Italian in the crew, asked Freeze.

"Nigga, who the hell you laughin' at? That car was bad ass!" Freeze looked over at Willie. "And I know you ain't laughing, 'cause you was the one showing off that south-side freak Gwangi, like she was some kinda catch. Every major nigga in the city tapped that ho, and you was walkin' 'round the mall, holding her hand and shit, like she was wifey material."

The whole table burst out in laughter.

"Nigga, you know I was just getting back in the city. I didn't know she was a freak like that. The bitch did give some good head though." Willie laughed, and everybody waited to see who was going to be the butt of the next joke.

Ken was glad to be back in the circle of bosses, his extended family. Every year, they gathered on Willie's yacht and caught up on old times. After borrowing money from all the men and running off, Ken was sure he'd never be able to enjoy such times again. Now, sitting amongst his colleagues, he was glad he'd decided to do the right thing.

"I remember last year when we came out here and Jones almost fell off the damn boat. Man, I miss that nigga," Jarvis,

G Street Chronicles / 217

recalling the eldest of the bosses, who had succumbed to a massive heart attack a few months earlier.

The laughter and smiles melted off of everyone's face at the mention of Jones, but Ken had trouble being too sad about it.

"Yeah, man, Jones is truly missed," he added, though he didn't mean a word of it; he owed Jones more money than he owed any of the others, and the man had taken his debt to the grave.

As the day wore on, *Jezebel* veered farther out into the ocean. The view was beautiful, nothing but blue water and sky all around.

"A'ight, y'all, let's pop some bottles and fire up some of this exotic stuff." Styles grabbed a bottle of Crown Royal and headed up to the deck.

All the men followed, and even the nonsmokers took a toke or two off the loud-smelling weed. They all stood around on the deck, looking out over the ocean, smoking and drinking.

Freeze pulled Jarvis to the side while the others made small talk. "It's time. His body will never make it back to land. The sharks will smell the blood and have him for dinner," he whispered as they cut their eyes in Ken's direction.

Oblivious, Ken was drinking, smoking, and laughing it up with the others.

Jarvis walked over and got everybody's attention. "Hey, listen up! It's time we deal with our brother Ken and square everything up so there wont be any misunderstandings."

Everyone gathered around him, and everyone but Ken knew exactly what time it was.

"Kenny boy, it's time to take care of everybody now," Jarvis said, cut his eyes to the silent bosses.

"Okay. One minute." Excited to have the burden off his chest,

Ken rushed off to get his bag, which he'd stashed downstairs, next to the table. In no time, he was back on deck. "All right, here we go." He reached inside his bag like Santa Clause, ready to pass the marked stacks off to each man. He'd added an extra $500 to each, just to drum up a bit of good will between them. After everyone was paid, he apologized again.

Jarvis patted the man on the back, a man he'd known for years. "That was a real noble move, Ken, and I truly commend you for it. However, as you know, you still violated and crossed certain lines, and that can't be forgiven with money. We accepted you back here today so you can pay each and every one of us, and you've only paid part of your debt. Now you'll pay the rest."

Right on cue, Willie pulled his .45 automatic from his waist.

Ken was totally confused by Jarvis's words, but he understood everything more clearly when he looked up and saw Willie pointing the gun at him. He started shaking all over. "But I paid my debt, y'all…even extra," he said, looking around at the blue water, knowing there was nowhere to run. He cursed himself for being so naïve, for trying to make amends with men like them. Now he wished he had taken Zo's advice and left town.

"Time to pay up, scandalous nigga!" With that, Willie pulled the trigger three times, knocking Ken backward, over the rail.

A second later, Ken splashed into the ocean, and a pinkish-red pool began to form around him. Within minutes, a frenzy of fins circled him, and everyone on the boat watched the grisly scene unfold, like something out of a horror film.

"Now you gonna walk the plank, muthafucka!" Willie said, standing behind all the men as they watched the sharks sink their razor-sharp teeth into Ken's flesh, tearing him apart. "Get off my boat!"

Everybody turned around and looked at Willie, who was now pointing the gun in their direction. The whole crew then circled around Jarvis the way the sharks had circled Ken.

"Huh? Wh-what y'all up to? What the fuck's going on?" Jarvis asked, confused while turning around in circles in the middle of the men.

Freeze spoke up as they cornered him in. "Nigga, you told us that nigga was dead! We coulda been sitting ducks because of your carelessness…or was it a lie to cover your old friend's ass? You and Ken had a hidden agenda, and we're all in agreement that both of y'all gotta pay," Willie said firmly.

"Agenda? I ain't got shit going on! I took the word of my second-in-command, who told me Ken was taken care of. This is all news to me too! In no kind of way would I ever try to deceive the crew! Man, y'all, come on," Jarvis pleaded. Then he did the first thing that came to his mind: He tried to run.

Willie and Lucci snatched him up before he got too far and walked him over to the rail like a couple of pissed-off pirates.

Jarvis fought hard, trying to break away, but they were too strong, and it was no use. "Please, y'all! I ain't got shit to do wit' Ken!" he screamed as they lifted him up over the rail. "No! Please!" Jarvis's screams of distress went unheard, though, because they were out in the middle of the ocean.

Freeze joined the two men and helped them toss him over. When they didn't hear a splash, they looked over the side and saw that he'd latched on to the searchlight protruding out of the front of the large vessel. The cold, salty ocean water smacked him in the face as he held on for dear life.

"Gimme that," Freeze said, reaching for Willie's .38.

"Be careful, man. Don't go puttin' a hole in my *Jezebel*,"

Willie said.

Boom! Boom!

Freeze leaned over the rail and fired two shots.

The first missed, but the second hit Jarvis in the shoulder, causing him to lose his grip. His bloody wound alerted the family of sharks that they were about to get seconds, and they hurriedly surrounded Jarvis, who was flailing in the water. Seconds later, they pulled him under and tore him apart, limb by limb.

The yacht captain who'd been working with Willie for years peeked out of the cabin when he heard the loud screams. As soon as he saw that Willie was okay, he ducked his head back in. He was used to Willie discarding unwanted guests overboard in the middle of the ocean. He navigated the big vessel back to shore, the remaining crew returned to their drinking, smoking, and laughing, as if nothing had happened—all of them a little richer and two people lighter.

G STREET CHRONICLES
A LITERARY POWERHOUSE
WWW.GSTREETCHRONICLES.COM

CHAPTER 34

One month later…

I had filed a missing persons report and followed up with the police on several occasions. I had even reached out to Willie, who owned the yacht Jarvis was supposed to be on for his meeting. He told the police and me that Jarvis had shown up at the marina in a convertible BMW with two suitcases in the back, and there was a white woman driving the car. He claimed Jarvis told him he had some pressing matters to tend to but would be in touch, that he'd apologized for not being able to make the meeting. When the police questioned the other attendees, everyone gave them the same story.

From that point on, I waited, night after night, for him to come home. After weeks passed with no word, I figured something bad must have happened to him. The fact that Jarvis was missing did sadden me, but I was aware of the consequences that came with the kind of life he lived and the kind of work he did. Over time, my heart had become cold, and his disappearance didn't touch me that deeply. I had lost my parents already, and later in my life, Prime had walked out on me, the man my world centered around. Jarvis being missing or even presumed dead was just another tragic chapter in the fucked-up story of my life.

After a while, Jarvis had been missing for so long that the police had finally declared him deceased. I searched the house up and down and found all the paperwork and deeds to all of Jarvis's possessions, and I made arrangements to have all of it transferred into my name. I knew it wouldn't be long before a relative or one of his long-lost friends would show up trying to lay claim to his property, but no one ever did.

"Can you recommend an attorney who can help me sort all this out?" I asked Dan Senegal after thanking him again for his help with Prime's case.

"I can give you a number. I'll give this guy a rundown on the situation. You'll just have to pay his fee, as well as my referral fee. My heart is heavy for Jarvis. He wasn't just a past client. He was also a friend."

I missed Jarvis, but I had a life to live, and thanks to him, I had a multimillion-dollar beachfront home, a lavish condo, two other oceanfront properties, and six expensive automobiles—not to mention the $1.4 million I'd found in the safe I'd paid a locksmith to open.

* * * * *

The figure clad in all black crouched down behind the broken-down old Buick that sat on the side of the soul food diner Big was known to frequent every Sunday night.

Big wobbled across the lot after devouring two slabs of pork ribs, a baked potato, and two sides of macaroni and cheese. He'd topped it off with a slice of peach pie and a large tea. He'd been lying low since the trial, because the word on the street was that he was working with the police. He was now doing all his business on the outskirts of the city, only coming back through on occasion.

The figure scurried across the lot and ducked behind Big's car before he got there. When Big approached, the dark one rose up out of the darkness, startling him. "Snitch-ass nigga," the Reaper hissed, quickly getting Big's attention.

His eyes grew as big as golf balls when she pounced on him. She knew the area well and was aware that gunshots at that hour of the night in that section of the city would have the police en route in minutes, like flies to honey. Instead, she opted for two razor-sharp titanium knives, handpicked for the job. She worked the knives like a surgeon as she pierced and cut Big until he was soaked in blood.

"Fuck! No! Stop it, you li'l bitch! Unh!" he cried. He tried to fight her, but the soon-to-be fatal wound to his chest crumbled him to the ground.

When the big man collapsed and fell next to his car in a blubbery heap, the Reaper wiped the handle of her knives off and dropped them in the sewer drain. Then she dashed away from the scene, disappearing into the darkness.

*****

Prime sat in his half-million-dollar crib out in Buckhead, watching *American Gangster* and counting the money he'd collected from his four dope spots earlier. Out of the blue, his phone rang, and he was quick to pick it up. "Yo?"

"I know I get a bonus for that fat-ass nigga. Shit," the Reaper said as she cruised downtown in her cherry-red Audi.

CHAPTER 35

"Hey, Moe, what's up? How's Aunt Linda doing?" Fiz asked, looking in the mirror at the long scar that ran down the side of her face.

"Who this?" Moe asked as he sat on his back porch in the west side of Chicago, drinking a Corona and listening to the radio.

"Nigga, this is your cousin Fiz. Boy, don't tell me you done forgot about me," she said as she lifted her hand and ran it down the scar, thinking about the rent she hadn't been able to pay because of her leg injury that kept her out of work. Fiz was pissed and wanted revenge on everyone who was responsible for her current position.

"Oh shit! Fiz? What up, Lady Bug?" Moe said excitedly, calling his favorite li'l cousin by her childhood name.

"Nothing much. Just touching base with you 'cause I met this girl down here who knows your friend Trent. You still fuck with him?" she asked, turning away from the mirror, unable to look at the mark that had diminished her good looks.

"You know I do. He's my right-hand man these days. He almost got taken out a while back, when some niggas tried to dead 'im, but he only lost an eye. He all good now. Anyway, who knows him down there?" he asked curiously.

"A li'l young chick named Nikki," Fiz said, then waited to see if Moe recognized the name.

"Nikki? Hmm. Never heard of her. Who'd she used to run wit'?" he asked, running the name through his head over and over again.

"Check this out. She said she took Trent's car and found money and dope in it," Fiz said, certain that it would jar Moe's memory.

Moe slammed the Corona on the back porch table and stood up. "Say what? You got tabs on that bitch? She's the one who almost got my peeps killed, the li'l ho who used to stay with Fat Fat and Katasha. We been looking for her for the longest. Damn, she just disappeared off the scene. You tellin' me she in the ATL now?" Moe said, pacing the back porch.

"Yeah, she was here for a while, but now she's staying in Miami. I know exactly where she is," Fiz said, knowing she could possibly get revenge and some much-needed rent money out of the deal if she worked it the right way.

Moe picked up the Corona and finished it off. "Cuz, you stay right there. Lemme call you right back," he said, then clicked off the line. His hands shook as he quickly punched in Trent's number.

"Yo, what up, fam'?" Trent asked, exhaling the smoke from the Kush he was smoking with his young goons from his block.

Since being shot, Trent had been going hard in the streets, and he no longer gave a damn about anything or anybody.

He had cheated death, and he felt invincible, even if he was missing an eye. Almost being killed had turned him into a heartless individual. He still hadn't tracked Greedy down yet, and he only hoped he'd get to him before the Brown Bag Boys caught up with him for the beef that had been publicized all over the city. Greedy wasn't Trent's only target though; he really wanted the one person who'd caused it all.

"Bruh, you ain't gonna believe this shit. My cousin Fiz just hit me up from the A. Guess who she ran in to," Moe said, then paused.

"Who?" Trent asked, watching his young gunners slap-box in the middle of the street.

"That young bitch Nikki, the one who took your car from Fat Fat's crib," Moe said with malice in his tone.

The line went silent for a minute. Trent adjusted his eye patch and thought back on the day when his car, his money, and his dope were stolen—one of the worst days in his life. "Oh yeah? Where that bitch at, my nigga?" Trent inquired.

"My cuz says she was staying in Atlanta for a while, but now she's in Miami. Gimme a minute to call her and get the lowdown." Moe hung up, then called Fiz back as he watched the neighborhood freak sneak into the married reverend's back door for one of their usual rolls in the sack that always set the reverend back $50.

"Hello?" Fiz answered.

"I need all the info on this ho, 'specially where she's laying her head," Moe said, grabbing a pen and scrap of paper from the kitchen drawer.

Fiz hesitated. "Moe, your people gotta shoot me something for this info, 'cause this shit could get me fucked up. I'm putting myself on the line," she said as she thought about a good price for the info.

"I'll hit you right back," he said, hanging up and calling Trent.

"Well? What's the deal? Where's the bitch?" Trent asked, ready to get his just due.

"My cuz wants us to drop her a li'l something for the info," Moe said reluctantly.

"Drop her something? A'ight. Fuck it. I just want that bitch, so get ready to take a trip down South," Trent said as he walked to the corner store. "Just take it out of last night's pickup."

"Okay. I'll offer her a couple stacks. I'll hit you back in a minute," Moe said, then hung up with Trent and called Fiz back. "I can give you two stacks. We'll stop by your spot on the way down," Moe said as he walked in the house, getting ready to head to Miami by way of Atlanta.

"Okay, cool. I can work wit' that. I'll text you my address," she replied. She smiled from ear to ear. Not only was she going to pocket a little cash, but her revenge was about to be administered.

* * * * *

Prime lounged around in his lavish five-bedroom home, thinking about how close he was to meeting his quota. Jarvis's words ran through his head daily, and he knew they were true. That was why he'd stormed out of the hotel room that night without looking back. He planned to take the dope Jarvis gave him and take the game to the next level until he was able to provide the finer things in life. He was more angry at himself than anything for getting all caught up.

Prime shook his thoughts and calculated his last drop and

realized he'd finally met his quota. He told himself daily that when that quota was met, he'd return to Miami where Jarvis resided, so he could claim what he felt was rightfully his. He picked up his phone, scrolled down the call list, and pressed the number he was looking for.

* * * * *

"Hello?" I answered, happy and mad at the same time when I saw Prime's number on my caller ID.

"Hey, baby. You ready to come home now?" Prime asked, as if him disappearing like that and ignoring all my calls hadn't been a big deal.

I didn't know whether to cuss his ass out or just scream and tell him to come on. It really was hard for me to contain myself when I heard his voice for the first time in months. "So what? You just gon' walk out on me and come back thinking shit is cool? How could you just leave me like that?" I asked, with my voice cracking and my eyes watering.

He got silent for a minute, then blew into the phone. "It was something I had to do. I had no choice, baby. I had to deal with it at the time. I can't lie. I was hurt by what you were into, straight up, but I know you did what you had to for me, and that's what counts. I just wanna be able to give you what he's given you and more. I'm good now, baby, so tell Jarvis I got every penny we owe him, with interest," he said, his words drawing more tears from my eyes.

I looked down at the big diamond Jarvis had bought for me and slid it slowly off my finger. "I've got something to tell you," I said, trying to figure out where to start.

"What?" he asked snappily, as if he was expecting some

bad news.

I set the $100,000 ring on the table. "Jarvis isn't...he's not around anymore," I said, making it sound as if we'd just broken up.

"What you mean? What's going on? You still in Miami?" he asked, bombarding me with question after question.

"Well, yeah, but a lot has happened." I went on to tell Prime about all the events leading up to Jarvis's disappearance and me claiming all of his assets.

"Damn. There's some kind of foul shit going on. Sounds like he crossed the wrong people or something. But are you tellin' me you own all his shit now?" Prime asked, realizing I was now wealthy.

"Yeah, but...well, it's cool to have all this money and stuff, but like they say, money can't buy happiness. Don't get me wrong. I'm happy to live a life of luxury, but something's missing," I said softly, trying my best to explain exactly what I was feeling.

"What, baby? What's missing?" Prime asked softly.

"You, Prime. I miss you." I smiled as I wiped the single tear that clouded my eye.

"Not for long. I'll be there as soon as I can," he said in a serious tone.

"Okay," I said, smiling.

"I gotta take care of some business, and then I'll be on my way. Text me the address, Nikki. As soon as I finish up, I'll be there. Talk to you later. Love you," he said in a tone I remembered so well.

"Love you too," I replied, then ended the call and immediately texted him the address.

I thought about Jarvis and felt kind of bad. I had all kind of crazy stuff running through my head. I even worried that Jarvis might come back while Prime was in the house. I cleared my crazy thoughts, asked God to lead me, then got up and went from room to room, removing all of Jarvis's personal items and pictures. I was so happy to know Prime was coming to Miami, and I planned on making up for all the time Prime and I had lost, and I wanted our first night to together again to be the best night of his life—one neither of us would ever forget.

CHAPTER 36

The next day, Trent, Moe, and two of their gunners crossed over the Atlanta city limits after an all-night drive. Moe called Fiz as soon as they exited the highway two blocks from her apartment. They checked the address she'd given them, then followed the directions on the GPS. They pulled up to her spot a few minutes later.

"Hey, cuz!" Fiz called out as she opened the door to let them in. Her hips, ass, and thick thighs that jutted out in the black tights she was wearing had all the men, even her cousin, checking her out hungrily.

"What up, baby? I see you still lookin' good," Moe said, hugging her. "This Trent, Hog, and Tito."

She looked up at Trent and was surprised to see that he looked quite the same as she remembered him; the patch that covered his eye was the only flaw in his handsome features. "Hey, y'all. Trent, you know I remember you. You're still looking all handsome and shit. Why you standing there lookin' crazy, like you don't remember me?" Fiz asked, stepping aside to let them in.

"You just done grew the fuck up, girl. You know I remember you," he replied, making sure she picked up on his flirtatious look.

Fiz smiled at him, then got back to the business at hand. "The li'l girl staying with a nigga name Jarvis in Miami. I got all his info," she said, then waited on the promised $2,000 before she handed it over.

Trent looked over at Moe, who was already pulling the money from his pocket. He counted the money out and handed it to her.

"One sec'," Fiz said, then walked to the back to get the information. A moment later, she returned with a notepad. She tore a page off of it and handed it to them, the directions to Jarvis's crib, as well as his home phone number.

"This is all legit', right?" Trent asked with doubt in his voice.

Fiz shot him a hard glance. "Don't try me," Fiz said sternly.

"You know I'm fucking wit' you, girl," Trent said, giving Fiz another up-and-down look. "C'mon, boys. Let's ride," he said, then followed his two speechless gunners back out to the car.

"Y'all be careful. Call me, cuz!" Fiz said as they left. She wished she could be there, but she could only imagine how it would all play out, and when she did, she laughed wickedly.

* * * * *

After Prime finished tying up all his loose ends, he prepared for his trip to Miami. He stuffed his 9mm and a few outfits into a bag and looked at his phone to check the address once more before he took off. Before leaving the city, he made sure all his spots were well supplied. The navigation in his Range Rover gave him an 11:30 destination arrival time.

$$* * * * *$$

Moe started the drive, but halfway through it, Tito took the wheel, since he was the only other person in the car with license. They clocked the destination and figured they'd arrive around 11:20.

Trent was sitting in the passenger seat, thinking of the best and most painful way to administer his punishment.

"You good, nigga?" Moe asked as they rode down the long, empty highway.

"Yeah. I'm just thinkin' 'bout how to teach this ho a lesson," he said, adjusting the patch, even though it was already in place, something that had become a habit.

Hours later, they were exiting the highway, pulling into the Food Mart. Everyone yawned and pepped up as the car came to a stop in front of the gas station.

"We 'bout here. Y'all go on and piss and get right," Moe said, grabbing his gun from under his seat and tucking it in his waistband.

Everybody got out, used the bathroom, and got back in, then made quick work of concealing their weapons under their clothing.

"Let's go!" Trent called out, alert and ready.

They rode a few miles up the road, then made a left on Jarvis's street.

"Right there," Hog said, looking down at the address Fiz had written and back up at the number on the mailbox.

"Shit, this bitch living large. Call the house and ask for the nigga," Moe ordered, passing Hog his throwaway prepaid cell phone.

* * * * *

The ringing phone made me jump as I lay in bed watching *CSI Miami*. "Hello?" I answered, wondering who was calling the house phone at such a late hour.

"Hey, is Jarvis in?" the man on the other end asked.

I was sure the caller knew him well, since he had the home phone number. "Um, no. He's not here. Can I take a message?"

"This is his old friend, Charles. I've got a package for him. Is it okay for me to leave it for him? You'll need to make sure he gets it though. It's worth a lot of money, but I need to drop it off before I leave on my overseas trip. I'm sorry it's so late."

"No problem. That's fine," I replied, curious about the valuable package. "Just leave it on the doorstep, and I'll make sure he get it."

"Okay. Thanks," he said.

I clicked off the line.

Ten minutes later, I heard a car pull up front. I peeked out the blinds and saw a man walking up the driveway with what had to be the valuable package. He dropped it at the front door, got back in his car, and pulled off.

* * * * *

"It's a go. She's gonna grab it anytime now," Moe said as he got out of the car on the dark, tree-lined road where Hog, Trent, and Tito were waiting for him.

"I love it when a plan comes together," Trent said playfully as they crossed the street and crept through the yard of the million-dollar estate, ready to put their plan in motion.

They huddled right outside the door, out of sight, waiting for it to open.

* * * * *

As soon as *CSI* went to commercial, I slipped into my robe and headed downstairs to grab the package. I turned the alarm off, unlatched the chainlock, and opened the door.

* * * * *

Prime looked at the numbers on the houses as he drove down the dark street. When he reached the address he was looking for, he did a double-take, not because of the big, extravagant home but because he saw four men pushing their way into the house. He checked the address again and pulled over a few yards down. "What the fuck is going on?" he said to himself as he grabbed his cell phone. After calling three times and not getting an answer, he grabbed his gun from his bag and headed up to the house.

* * * * *

"No! Get outta my house! Please get out! What do you want anyway? Jarvis isn't even here!" I screamed, certain that they were looking for him.

"Bitch, shut up!" Moe screamed as he picked me up and slammed me to the floor.

"Unh!" the force of the slam knocked the wind out of me.

All the men circled around me as I lay there, curled up in a ball. As I focused on the men surrounding me, it became clear who one of them was and what they were really up to. "Tr-Trent?" I asked, and my heart skipped a beat.

He knelt down close to me and smiled. "So you remember me even with the patch, huh? Nice place you've got here. Seems you're doin' pretty damn well for yourself. But let me ask you something." He paused to pull his gun from his waistband. "Did you use my shit to help you pay for all this?" he asked sarcastically, then put the weapon right in my face.

"Please, Trent! I-I didn't know. I was just…I wanted to get away. I swear I didn't know what you had in the car," I tried to explain, but from the look on his face, he didn't want to hear it.

"Yeah, yeah. Well fuck that. When I called you and told you to bring my shit back, you ignored me and kept right on going. Seeing this spot, I know you and your dude got dough up in here, so turn it over," he said with aggression, pressing the gun in my cheek.

"Trent, I can get you money, way more than you lost. I just need to go to the bank in the morning. I swear!" I pleaded, suddenly recalling the day my parents were killed.

He looked at me, frowned, then turned his attention to the three men who were standing behind him. "Y'all search this muthafucker and take anything that's worth anything. I'm gonna sit here with Nikki. Seems me and my old friend have a little catching up to do," he said, then reached over and grabbed my chin and squeezed.

"Ow!" I screamed, pulling away. "Trent, I'll get money for you. Just please don't do this," I said calmly, hoping he would go along with me.

"Can you get this too?" he screamed, lifting up the patch and letting me see the dark hole where his eye used to be. "Can you replace my eye, Nikki? Huh!?"

I looked at him, lost for words.

He snatched me up by my hair.

"Please! God, no!" I screamed.

He lifted the gun and slammed it into the side of my head, knocking me back down.

"Ow!" I cried as I fell to the floor.

* * * * *

Prime watched the scene through the front window. He quickly scrambled up onto the porch and tried the font door, knowing that he was running out of time. He turned the knob, stepped in, and thought about Taj; he couldn't let another of his loves be brutally killed. He crept up in the foyer and eased around until he was a few feet from Trent.

* * * * *

"Man, ain't shit up in this bitch," Moe called out in frustration, entering the room and forcing Prime to dip behind the sofa, out of sight.

"I had something special planned for you," Trent said, "but since time won't permit, I'ma make this short and sweet." He cocked the gun.

"Yo, there's a safe in here!" Hog yelled from upstairs.

"Grab her," Trent told Tito as he came back on the scene with a handful of my jewelry.

They picked me up, but before we got to the steps, shots rang out.

Pop! Pop! Pop!

Hog fell forward, right next to Tito, whose head was spewing blood.

"Oh shit!" Trent yelled, then took off upstairs.

Moe ran to the back, and I scrambled away, trying to see where the shots were coming from.

"Get down, Nikki!" Prime screamed, running over to me.

Pop! Pop!

Two shots barely missed me as we ran for cover.

"Prime? Where...how'd you...thank you, God!" I said, hugging him tight.

When we heard the back door open, we broke our embrace. In an instant, Prime took off behind Moe, who was fleeing on foot. Moe ran hard across the yard, but before he could clear the grass, he slipped and tumbled.

Prime was on him instantly. "Fuck nigga!" Prime spat, leveling the gun.

"Man, Fiz sent us! Man, we ain't—"

Pop!

His words were cut short by the blast of the gun. His head rocked back onto the wet grass.

Prime retreated back into the house. As soon as he stepped in the door, he came face to face with Trent, whose hand was around my neck. He had his gun pointed at my head.

"Hold up, man. Just let her go. It's over," Prime said calmly, then laid his gun on the floor.

I felt Trent shaking, and nervous sweat was running down his face.

"This shit ain't over till I say it's over!" Trent screamed as he pulled the trigger, hitting Prime.

I made a break for it, pulling away and running back through the house.

"Bitch, you dead!" Trent turned around slowly, knowing I was cornered.

NIKKI

I ran upstairs to my bedroom with Trent walking behind me, laughing like a madman. When I got in my room, I grabbed the phone, but before I could call 911, he was at the door. I dropped the phone and got in the closet. I pulled the door closed and got behind the hanging clothes.

He continued to laugh like some kind of deranged, one-eyed serial killer as he made his way over to the closet. Seconds later, the door swung open, and a single shot rang out.

Boom!

Then, just like that, everything went quiet. When I looked out, I saw Trent lying there, spread eagle, with a big hole in his chest from the 12-gauge I was still holding shakily in my hands. I laid the gun down and ran, as fast as I could, down the stairs.

Prime was lying in the front of the house, holding his flesh wound that had nicked a piece of meat out of his thigh.

"Oh my God! Prime, are you okay?" I said, helping him up.

"Yeah. Let's get the fuck outta here though," he called out in pain.

I ran to the bathroom to get him something to wrap his leg, and it reminded me of that time long ago, when I'd fetched warm, wet towels for the injuries Rude Boy had left on his face.

Minutes later, we were on the highway, on our way back to Atlanta. It was hard to leave that lavish life behind, the one I'd prayed for all my life, but I was willing to go anywhere with Prime, who'd saved my life all over again.

CHAPTER 37

Two months later…

"**G**irl, this is nice! I'm so happy for you!" Jareka told Fiz as they toured Exotic Styles, Fiz's new hair salon that Vince, her new sugar daddy, had helped her to open.

Fiz and Jareka had become fast friends after meeting one night in the club. When Jareka had asked about a waitressing job, Fiz had convinced her to try her dancing skills on the pole. The first night, she made close to $1,000, and that impressed her quite a bit. Jareka was a little rough around the edges, but after a complete makeover, her petite, curvy figure, short, Amber Rose blonde cut, and pretty smile had all the ballers trying to get with her.

"Yeah, girl, my Grand Opening's gonna be crunk," Fiz said, proud of her accomplishments.

"Yeah, I bet! Where's the bathroom with all the gold fixtures you told me about?" Jareka asked.

"Oh, you're gonna love it!" Fiz said excitedly as she led

the way to the back. "Ta-day!" she called out, but when she looked up and saw her friend's maniacal reflection in the mirror, brandishing a gleaming weapon, she instantly began to scream.

Jareka brought the sharp blade down across the back of her neck, then spun her around and buried it in her chest with one quick motion.

Fiz fell over the new marble sink and slid down to the marble floor tiles, coating them with crimson.

Jareka closed the door behind her and eased out of the shop. As soon as she got in the car, she pulled out her cell phone. "It's done," she told Prime as she headed out to his new spot.

She pulled up outside of the house and parked, knowing I was home alone. Ever since the night they'd spent together years earlier, after Prime had witnessed her pulling a job for Zulu, who was now serving time for the same murder, Jareka had been earning her nickname, putting in work for Prime, hoping he'd eventually make good on his promise that the two of them would one day become an item. After taking out Rude Boy and Banta Man for killing Taj, the Reaper was sure Prime would fall into her arms in gratitude and love. Now she sat outside his house, wiping away bitter tears, because Prime had a new love interest and only called her when he wanted her to put in work. "Fuck this shit," the Reaper said as she pushed her car door open, sticking to her word to kill every bitch Prime had made his; she only wanted him to be hers.

Ding! Dong!

"Coming!" I said, feeling great in my new life, eagerly awaiting the birth of mine and Prime's baby.

G STREET CHRONICLES
PRESENTS

We'd like to thank you for supporting G Street Chronicles
and invite you to join our social networks.
Please be sure to post a review when you're finished reading.

Like us on Facebook
G Street Chronicles
G Street Chronicles CEO Exclusive Readers Group

Follow us on Twitter
@GStreetChronicl

Follow us on Instagram
gstreetchronicles

Email us and we'll add you to our mailing list
fans@gstreetchronicles.com

George Sherman Hudson, CEO
Shawna A., COO